KENDRICK

VALLEY OF WOLVES BOOK 2

KATHI S. BARTON

This is a work of fiction. Names, characters, places, and incidents are products of the author's imagination or are used fictitiously and are not to be construed as real. Any resemblance to actual events, locations, organizations, or persons, living or dead, is entirely coincidental.

World Castle Publishing, LLC
Pensacola, Florida
Copyright © 2026 Kathi S. Barton
Hardback ISBN: 9798243385053
Paperback ISBN: 9798891265066
eBook ISBN: 9798891265073
First Edition World Castle Publishing, LLC, February 2, 2026
http://www.worldcastlepublishing.com
Licensing Notes
Cover: Cover Designs by Karen
Editor: Karen Fuller

Prologue

Sharon didn't know what to do about her hand and getting out of work. She'd been able to get out of the blind date, thankfully, and now she had to figure out how she was going to go to her job while being bandaged up like she was.

"You can run the register." She supposed that she could expect to bag things up. "You'll be fine. I can do the rest, and we just won't have any sammiches for the day. I'll have one of the others come in and slice the meat up, and I'll make them in between customers if it comes to that. You got yourself some pain pills, don't you?"

"I do, but they make me woozy a little bit." Daff, an apt name if she'd ever heard one, said that she'd make sure that she was up on her feet. "I just don't want to cause you any more trouble than I already have."

"This is my shop, and I do what I want. You don't have to do anything with the people getting gas, so that's gonna be all right. You just ring them out, and we'll have a productive day today." She said she'd try not to do too much that would cause her to do double work. "You just be you, honey. You'll see that people can be kind when they wanna. I know a few people around here who sets stock in you."

She had no idea what that meant, but let it go. Sometimes, having Daff explain something was worse than having her just say it and move on. So here she was, running the register in the busiest part of the day, hoping to goodness that she could get a break soon so she could pee. Another hard job when you only had one hand to adjust and pull up your pants.

"Should you be working?" She'd heard that at least a dozen times today and always just nodded and said she was fine. Daff was doing a good job of keeping her from using her hand a great deal. When someone came into the shop, and they had pops and more stuff than they could carry, she'd have them bagged up and out the door sometimes before they got their change.

By lunch, she'd had enough and only wanted to sit down and have a break with a pain pill. Taking half of one was almost as bad as taking a whole one, but it did take the pain away for a little while. Coming out of the back room, she saw the doctor who had helped her last night.

"I wanted to check on you and see how you were doing. Should you be here?" She explained to him how she wasn't doing anything but running the register for the place and that Daff had the rest under control. "I did notice last night that she seems to know what she's doing. Today, I'm headed home. I was at the hospital until all hours last night, and all I want to do is check on you and make sure you're all right, then head home."

"I'm sure that the hospital was happy for your help. I know that I was when you came in." She thought the man was about as handsome as she'd ever met. Even as tired as he looked, he looked good enough to snack on. Embarrassed, she changed the subject. "My hand doesn't hurt too badly right now. I know that they had to put in a lot of stitches in it, and I'm grateful for what you did for me."

"It wasn't anything. Just getting the wound closed so that you'd stop bleeding was first and foremost. Then, once you were at the hospital, they got it cleaned up and sealed for you. You're lucky you didn't lose a finger. I hope you're more careful next time." She thought that he looked embarrassed and smiled a little. "Anyway, I just wanted to check on you and see how you're doing."

He looked hesitant to leave. She didn't mind him hanging around, so when the next customer came in, she dealt with him and the next two afterwards. She was ringing out the next customer when he suddenly asked her if she'd like to have dinner with him.

"I mean, I know that we can't go to a steak

house. You'd be hard-pressed to cut up yours, but I could do it. It won't be like a blind date for us since we know one another. Sort of. I'm Kendrick Valley. I'm a medical doctor at Dresden and the local hospital. And you're Sharon." She told him her last name. "Sharon Taylor. It's lovely to meet you."

"Same from me." She felt silly again and rang out a couple more people. "I'd love to have any kind of dinner with you. And you're right. It wouldn't be like a blind date. Besides, I don't have any bad books I can read at the moment." They both laughed.

"Would tonight be all right with you? I'd understand if you just wanted to go home and rest your hand with some pain medication. We can do it some other night this week." She said that she really was all right and wanted to have dinner with him. "I have a better idea. How about I pick up some pizza tonight, and then we can have dinner together on Friday night. That should be better for your hand and me getting a good day's sleep in. I'll call you too. If that's all right?"

"It would be perfect. I love pizza." She really did, too, and was glad that he suggested it so that she could rest her hand, too. It really wasn't feeling as great as she said it was, and she was sure that he knew it. "I'll write down my address for you, and since you don't know the pizza places around here, I'll order one for us so that we can get to know one another. What do you think of that?"

"Perfect." She gave him her address and a time. She'd order the pizza and make sure that it was delivered on time. When he reached for the piece of paper, their hands brushed one another, and she felt a tingling that she'd never experienced before. It was like a connection or something. After he left her. She did wonder what he was going to do for the rest of the day while he waited around for her to get off work.

~*~

Kendrick knew that she was his mate, but wasn't at all sure how to go about telling her that he was a wolf and that she was his other half. He didn't even know if she knew what a shifter was. She hadn't smelled like anyone that could shift had been around her, but then she had been covered in a good amount of blood, and that could have been it. It had taken him at least two hours to figure out why he kept getting drawn back to the area that she'd been in, and then it hit him. She was his mate. Kendrick thought about what his brother would say if he were to tell him.

They'd make fun of him is what would happen. They were relentless in their teasing of Conri, and he was their alpha. They'd be terrible with him if they found out, and he just didn't want to hear it. Not until he got to know her better, anyway. Besides, he might well be mistaken.

"Nah, she's the one. You knew it last night and then today, moron." He put gas in his car and paid at the pump so as not to get in her hair again. But damn, but he wanted to. He felt the need to heal her, too. To make her pain, which was pushing at him, to make go away, too. "I'll tell her tonight when I see her. I'll just set her down and tell her that I'm a wolf shifter and that I'm mated to her. That should be good."

It wasn't good that he was talking to himself again. He only did that when he was nervous, and he was very nervous right now. Going back to the hotel that he'd rented this morning, he decided to go and find a place where he could get himself some jeans and some other things to change into. He didn't want to smell like blood, which he could smell on himself when having a date with his other half. He kept telling himself that. That he'd seen and met his other half and would spend the rest of his life with her.

He found a Walmart not far from where he was staying. Getting himself some jeans and other things that he was going to need, he put them all in a cart and made his way to the front of the store. He thought about getting a case of water; he did need one at home, but he thought about dragging it all the way back with him and decided that he'd get it later. Right now, it was up in the air about when he was going to go back home. He had a practice, sure, but he'd cleaned the next two days for himself so that he could get to know Sharon.

While in line, he found himself a book. It was one that he'd not read yet, and he tossed it into his cart. He had lots of time to waste between now and five-thirty and didn't want to seem like a stocker by hanging around at the gas station. He didn't want to scare her off before he'd even gotten to meet her.

Going back to the hotel, he took a long, hot shower and changed into his new clothing. Shaving, too, he felt at least a little better about going out now and sat down on his bed to start on his book. It was hard for him to get into it because he kept thinking that he was going to forget the time, and he finally set an alarm. Fat lot of good it had done him.

He kept making sure that he'd set the alarm right. When that was correct, he had to make sure that his phone was charged up and wouldn't die when he needed it to remind him when to go. Christ, this was worse than when he was studying for his exams. He'd been checking on things so much that he nearly overslept when he finally fell asleep in his dorm room.

At some point, he fell asleep and was awakened by the alarm that he had set correctly. Getting up and brushing his teeth, and combing his hair, he was ready to leave when his cell phone rang. It was Sharon. Sitting down, just knowing that she was going to cancel, he answered the phone with his name.

"It's Sharon. Sharon Taylor. I wanted to let you know that the pizza isn't going to be delivered because they're short-staffed at the moment, and I wondered if you could pick it up on your way to my house." He said that he could do that and wrote down the address. "They said it would be all right if you picked it up and that I ordered it. The people there know that I order all the time and were worried that I was getting myself into something bad. So if they give you the fifth degree, that's why. They're slightly overly protective of me."

"Good. You need to have someone watch over you sometimes. Right?" She said she supposed so and told him she'd see him in a little while. Just before she hung up, she asked him if he liked beer or tea with his pizza. "Both, but I'll stick to tea with you. You don't want to be drinking with those pain pills they gave you."

"It's funny, but after seeing you today, I've not had a bit of pain today. It's like it's all healed up." He had not thought that his touching her might do that. "All right, I'll see you soon. I'm really looking forward to this tonight."

"So am I. I'll see you soon, Sharon." Leaving the hotel, he was on his way to the pizza place in a few minutes. As soon as he arrived and told them who he was picking up for, they did ask him a lot of questions.

They didn't seem impressed with him being a doctor because, of course, doctors could be predators, too.

"I know your name now, so you'd be better off behaving yourself. I like Sharon, and she's a good girl. A little on the shy side, but she's a good girl to everyone." He promised the owner of the pizza place that he'd be on his best behavior. "See that you do. I'm not opposed to killing you if you hurt her."

"I'd allow you to do that, too, if I were to harm a hair on her head. She means a great deal to me as well." One of the others whispered in his ear, and the boss looked at him. Then he leaned over the counter and asked him if he was a wolf. "I am. And if you know that, you know that as my mate, I won't harm her at all. I'm going to talk to her tonight about it."

He nodded before speaking again. "You see that you do. And I don't want to hear about you taking advantage of her just because she's your mate, either. I know that it's rare, but you behave yourself too. Like I said, she's a good girl."

"I promise you on the heart of my mother, she'll be as safe with me as she would be with you." That seemed to satisfy him, and he handed over the pizza. "Call it a pre-wedding gift for the two of you. Now get on out of here before it gets cold. Pizza...my pizza isn't good cold. You eat it hot or not at all."

"Thank you." He didn't even feel jealous about

the man drilling him about Sharon. He was glad that someone was out there watching over her for him. And when he got to the house, he was very glad when she asked who it was before opening the door to him. Yes, she was going to be safe with him forever.

"This is the best pizza, wouldn't you agree?" He said that he'd never had one better. I never thought to ask you if you'd like a meat one. But then, I guess you eat a great deal of meat." He asked her what she meant. "Grizzle called here after you left the pizza shop. He told me to have an open mind and that you were a shifter. A wolf shifter. And that you had something to talk to me about. Is that all true?"

"It is. And since I'm assuming you're not flying off the handle or anything, you know what you are to me." She nodded and suddenly found her pants interesting. "Look at me, Sharon. I won't ever hurt you. Not in any way."

"I know that. I don't know why I know that, but I do. Also, you healed my hand for me, didn't you?" He said that he didn't know. He'd never had a mate before and didn't know what he could do with just a touch. "It doesn't hurt at all. I've been tempted to pull the bandages off and look for myself, but I'm afraid of what I might see. Is that something that mates are supposed to be able to do to each other?"

"I don't know, honestly. What I do know is that

today, when you passed me the note with your address on it, I felt something tingle. Did you feel anything?" She told him that she'd felt the same thing. "Then I can only assume. If it's not healed up, I can put the bandages back on you. I never go without my medical bag. I even filled it out today when I was at the store. I'm always afraid of not having what I need the next time, so I always do that when I'm...I'm babbling. I want to see it, too."

She undid the wrap and, with shaking hands, showed him what was left of her wound. Just black threads in the wrapping and nothing more. Even the cut looked healed. The scar was still pink, but it was about as good-looking as if it had happened months ago instead of last night. He kissed the area, and she inhaled sharply.

"You're beautiful, Sharon." She slid to the floor with him, and he kissed her again. This time on the mouth. "You're so very beautiful that I'm excited for the next thousand years or so hanging out with you."

"That's a long time." He'd tell her later that they had that much and more to be together. Tonight was for them. "I'm not much of a catch, I'm afraid. Daff was allowing me to work so that I could have some income. She's good to me."

"You won't have to worry about money again, love. I have enough for us." She nodded, and he smiled.

"Can I kiss you again? You taste like pizza and beer, and that's so good."

He had to calm his wolf a couple of times when they got into kissing heavily. As soon as she got up to clean up their mess, he had a good talk with himself and his wolf. He didn't want to make love to her on the night he promised to behave himself. No, he was going to be a good man and woo her first.

"I have some dessert. I have apple pie and lemon refrigerator cake. Which do you want?" Two of his favorites, how was he to choose? It was going to be difficult being a good man with a woman who spoke to his inner beast.

Chapter 1

Going home after spending the evening with Sharon, Kendrick decided that he'd move to any place that she wanted and damn the fact that he had a pretty good practice right now. Being a doctor of good standing, he knew that he could get a job anywhere and be happy so long as she was. It was his life's mission to make his mate happy in every way possible. Boy, did he sound sappy right then, and he had to laugh at himself. His brothers would be teasing him forever about how they'd met. And he found that he was all right with that as well.

She'd been working when he'd gone into the gas station to thank the owner for letting him leave his car parked in their lot all day. He'd been hanging out with Conri and Cass for the day at Rainersville for the big traders/swappers days they had every year, and had asked to park his car there rather than drive behind them. As it turned out, he was glad that he had as Sharon, Sharon Taylor had been hurt on the slicer and needed fifty-four stitches when the meat she'd been slicing had fallen over, and the slicer had cut her up badly.

Taking her to the hospital in an ambulance, he'd gotten rooked into staying until three in the morning, helping with other patients that had come in from all kinds of ailments after spending the day out in the sun. Taking a nap in the hospital so he could drive home, he had stopped into the gas station again to make sure that Sharon was all right. He didn't know immediately that she was his mate, but it didn't take him long to ask her out.

They had pizza for their first date, and he couldn't have been happier. When her wound was suddenly healed from his touching her, he knew then without a doubt that she was his mate. His healing her sort of sealed the deal for them, he thought.

Now that he was home and working, he wanted to close up shop and go to see her again. They had talked a great deal when he'd been with her, but nothing earth-shattering. She told him she was as poor as a church mouse, and he told her that she didn't have to worry about money ever again.

"I will forever worry about money even if I have a billion dollars." He told her how sorry he was for being so flippant about money. "Just keep that in mind, as well as I'm not going to be a kept woman. I like to work. Not as hard as I am right now, but I don't think I could stay at home and be pampered for the rest of my life." She looked at him before speaking again. "Okay, that's not true. I could be pampered by the right person, but I need to make sure that I don't become as large as a house waiting for my husband or whatever to come home to me."

"You'll never gain any weight unless you're breeding or having children. Nor will human illnesses claim your life. I only need to claim you as my mate so that you'll live a very long and hopefully stitches-free life." She laughed, and that was what he'd been hoping for. "Also, no matter if you're on the pill or other kinds of contraceptives, you'll get pregnant if you're ovulating if we have sex. If we have children, I mean."

"*If* we have children?" He told her that he believed that since it was her body and only hers, she would decide when they had children and sex. "I'd like to believe that, but I've been around before. I'm not saying that you're lying to me, but—"

"That's another thing. I can't lie to you. Not that I would, but it's something in my DNA that prevents me from telling you a lie or even by omission. To me, it's the same as a lie." She just eyed him hard. "I swear to you on the heart of my mother, who is alive and well, that I'm telling you the truth. And so you know, if you ask me something, I'm not going to be able to sugarcoat it as much as you might like."

"Do I look fat to you?" He said he thought that

she was a beautiful creature and that he was already half in love with her. "Good answer. I don't know about the love part yet, but I like that you can't lie to me. It might just save your ass if anything comes up like another woman."

"There won't be. Ever. I promise you." They talked about him being a wolf, and she asked him some good questions. When it got to his age, he told her how old he was, and he wasn't sure she had believed him. He was honest in telling her that he was nearly four hundred years old, only younger than his older brother, Conri, by a few years. "I've been waiting for you for all my life."

"I don't have much in the way of family left. My mom and dad are still alive, but I've not spoken to either of them for a decade. Mom lives in California, and my dad lives in upstate New York. I hadn't thought of it before, but they couldn't be more apart than they are right now. They've been divorced since I was about ten and have never gotten along well enough to allow me to live with either of them. I lived with my grandma until she had to go into a nursing home." He asked if her parents were happy. "I don't know whether they understand that word or not. They seem to be their happiest when they're bickering with each other. I just stay out of their way. They don't bother me, and I do the same for them. To be honest, I don't know that I'd recognize them if they were to come up to me on the street. I hate to think about that, but that's the way I feel."

"I'm sorry. Our father was a bastard. He and my brother Conri's first wife had an affair and stole from the pack. Since he never claimed her, she wasn't immortal like we are. Mom took her immortality from dad when it was figured out what he'd been doing, and she's never been happier." She said that it sounded like neither of them had had a good childhood. "If not for my mom, I might well believe that. She was our rock and foundation at the same time."

"I believe in those kinds of families. However, I've never experienced one. My grannie is all right, a little off her noodle at times, but I love her. She's in a state-run nursing home, and they treat her fairly well. I go and see her when I can. She no longer remembers who I am, and that's sad, but I know her, so that's all right." He asked if she was happy. "Am I happy? I don't know that I ever thought about that before. I have a place where I live. It's not great, but it's a roof over my head. I have food when I want it and am glad that my landlord is so forgiving at times. But other than that, it's fine."

"I want to see about making you happy." She told him that she was just fine, and that bothered him somewhat. She seemed resigned to the fact that she had the essentials and that was all that she needed. Perhaps it was, he thought with a smile. She might have the right way to go about life, like she was.

He'd been like that a few hundred years ago. Bored with life, he'd gone through the motions of the day and did nothing else. Not even to interact with his family. His mother had told him that he needed a hobby of some sort, and that was when he became a doctor for the first time. Since working in the hospital at the time, it was easy enough for him to get his degree as a doctor and help those around him. He thought, too, that his brother Yanick was suffering from that now and needed something to shake up his life. He'd have to get on him about that before he became too set in his ways.

Today, he had a full day of seeing patients. His first one was an elderly woman who had been around as a child while he'd been living here. She was forever telling him how he'd babysat her as a child, and he told her she'd been a naughty child. They had fun, the two of them, and he thought that was the hardest part of being around forever. You saw people who were children grow up and get old. It was hard on the heart, he told her.

"What brings you in today, Mary?" She said that her blood pressure medicine had expired and that she needed to see him in order to get her new prescription.

"I can do that. When will you run out of it?"

After taking her blood pressure and telling her that she was doing well, he took some blood to make sure that her counts were still reading all right. She was just telling him about her garden and how she had the biggest carrots this year when his nurse came in to find him. After excusing himself, he went out to see what she wanted.

"There is the little Allen boy back to see you. He said that his rash isn't getting any better. I'm thinking that he's getting into it daily and doesn't know any better. I heard that his momma was having the vines taken off their house. Could be that it's poison ivy." He asked if she'd make sure that his chart was up to date. "I can do that. But you should see this boy. He's a mess. I'd say he's taking a shower in the vines if I didn't know any better."

After doing a quick exam of Jason, he went back to Mary. She was concerned about the little fella and told him so. After assuring her that he was going to take care of them both. He renewed her prescription and sent her on her way. But not before he had a large bag of carrots that he was going to be taking to his mom's house tonight.

By lunchtime, he'd had Jason taken care of and sent him home with something stronger and a stern warning about what poison ivy looked like. He was nursing a few places that were raw, and he was concerned about them. If they continued to be raw like they were, he was going to have to put him in the hospital for a couple of days on something stronger to get him taken care of. He had a bad reaction.

Eating his lunch of cold pizza, which he'd brought from home, he messaged Sharon about his day so far. He didn't want to call her and disturb her work, and knew that she'd answer him when she got a few minutes. He didn't want to distract her while using the slicer either. That was a dangerous piece of equipment. Since she'd been cut so badly and had already healed, she had to continue to wear the bandage so that no one freaked out. But since she didn't hurt anymore, it was easier for her to go back to work.

By the time he'd been ready to go home, he'd seen another three children with bad cases of poison ivy. He was going to have to have his brother check to see where the epidemic was coming from and see if he could put a stop to it. If they were to burn the vines, he'd have even more trouble with infections, and he'd just as soon stop it if he could. He had a feeling that they were 'helping' and getting the ivy all over their skin.

He thought about driving up to see Sharon again, but she had left him a message that she was coming to see him. Kendrick was excited about that.

Most of his house was in flux because he was moving again, but he thought that if she had time, they could look at houses together.

Kendrick and his brothers moved to a different house every ten to fifteen years just so they'd not be too set in their ways. It was a good way to stave off boredom as well. He'd been looking at houses for the past month and had narrowed it down to three of them. Sharon knew that was one of the things that he wanted to do with her, and also to meet his family. She was nervous about meeting them. Especially his mom and older brother.

Conri was the alpha of the pack, and she'd never met one before. He'd tried telling her that he was like a big cuddly dog, but she wasn't having it. Just the idea that he could have the pack kill her by his word scared her to death. He'd never thought about it before and was glad that he'd told his brother not to go too overboard in meeting her. He didn't want her scared of him.

By the time she arrived, he'd cleaned his place up as best he could and made and discarded two different lists of homes she might want to see. He wanted to live near his family, but she might want to be closer to her job. Whatever she wanted, he was going to be there for her. Stretching when she pulled into the driveway, he watched her pull into one of the spaces in front of the garage and get out.

Rushing out to help her in, he was surprised that she had brought a bag with her of clothing. He didn't want to read too much into it, so he said nothing when he took it from her and into the house. Kendrick explained how he was in the process of moving, and the things that he was taking with him were packed up. The rest would be sold with the house, or he'd have an auction to get rid of the things he was starting fresh with.

"We'll get to start fresh in a new place if we find one you like." She told him she'd never lived in a house before. "I've always lived in a house. I'm assuming you mean apartments when you say that."

"Grannie had a trailer that was as old as dirt when I moved in with her. My parents both barely afforded an apartment when they were getting a divorce. I have a one-bedroom, as you've seen, that isn't all that much." He told her he thought it was cozy. "It is. Too cozy. But I think I'd like to look at houses with you. Just don't expect me to have much of an opinion about them. I know very little about living in a one-family structure."

After having something to tie them over until dinner time, she sat in his living room and looked around. He tried to see what she was seeing, and all he could see was a few boxes and things that he'd been living in for the last fifteen years.

"You're very wealthy, aren't you?" He sat down before answering. "I've looked you up. Not just you, but your family. There is a lot out there on the things that you've done for your area."

"We're very generous with our money, yes." She nodded, then looked around the room again. "I feel like you're building up to something, and I don't know what it is. If you could help me out, I'd not feel so out of my depth."

"Daff, my boss, you met her the other day, she said that she knows of you guys as well, and said that you have stupid money. I wasn't sure what she meant by that until she explained it. It means that you can be stupid with your money, and it wouldn't put a dent in what you have. Is that true?" He told her that he'd not do anything stupid with money, but he supposed that it was true. "I thought you'd say that. I've left my job. Daff said I'd be stupid to keep working at a shit job when you could take care of me. Besides, she said that it wasn't fair of me to have that kind of stupid money and work for her too. She gives jobs to people who are down on their luck, like I was."

"So she fired you." Sharon nodded but still wouldn't look at him. "There's more, right? More you're working up to telling me."

"In addition to losing my job, I lost my place to

stay as well. That was more straightforward than me just losing my job. He found out that I was going to be married to you and jacked up my rent to about four times what I was paying. I got into an argument with him, and without the help of Daff, I wouldn't have left with what I have. Just my clothing. The place was furnished anyway."

"Do you want me to take care of him for you?" She eyed him then, and he didn't so much as blink at her. "I can. You just tell me where he lives, and I'll get whatever else you want from the place within the hour."

"Would you kill him if I told you that he hurt me? Not physically but mentally?" He just stared at her, telling her that he'd do what he felt was necessary. "I see. He just hurt my feelings, nothing more. I didn't expect to be treated the way that I had over someone else's money."

"What I have now belongs to you. Everything that I have, or will have in the future, is now yours." She told him that she didn't want that. "It's done. I called the bank this morning and had your name put on all my credit."

"What if I have a terrible credit score? Aren't you afraid that it will bring down your number, too?" He said that he had enough cash lying around that it wouldn't matter to him one way or the other. "You're nuts."

"Thank you. But I will take care of your landlord, and no one will ever find his body." She looked frightened, and he told her that he'd never harm her. "I swear to you that he'll be all right so long as he doesn't piss me off too."

"You're scary when you're all macho." She took his hand into her much smaller one. "I don't have a place to live. May I help you find a place for us to live and stay here with you? I promise not to be a bother. I need a job too."

"You're very welcome to stay with me forever. As for a job, I don't know of any right now, but I can keep an ear out for one for you. Also with the pack." She said that she didn't want to rush into anything right away; her feelings were still tender from the landlord. "I'll gladly show him the error of his ways if you'd allow me to. I can't promise that I won't hurt him, but I'll gladly make sure he understands that to hurt you in any way hurts me."

"I'll be fine. I think I was just too tender at the moment since Daff had fired me. Gently, of course, she was so nice that I wanted to fire myself when she pointed out that I was taking the job of someone who needed it. So he might have been nice, and I wasn't feeling it." He said he understood. "Can I have my own bedroom for now? I don't want to sound ungrateful about you allowing me to live here, but I'm not ready for sex just yet."

"Of course." He took her to the two bedrooms on the second floor and let her choose. His bedroom was at the other end of the hall, and he promised her that he didn't get up much during the night unless he was on call. "There is a washer and dryer up here as well as one on the first floor that you can use if you wish as well."

It worked out for the two of them in that he showed her around and made plans with his family to have dinner at one of their homes. It was Cass who said she'd host dinner, and then he told her about her losing her job and place to live today. Telling her that she was tender didn't get him teased at all when he thought for sure that it would have.

~*~

She couldn't have asked for a better family to hang out with. Cass told her how welcome she was and that the two of them hit it off so well that it surprised her. She didn't make female friends so easily, and she was glad for the friendship of the other woman. The men were nice, too, and overly polite. It occurred to her that wolves might be the jealous type, and that was why they were keeping their distance from her. She asked Cass about it.

"You're newly mated to Kendrick and have not

yet bonded. They are a jealous lot, but can be as sweet as pie, too, when they want to be. I think that's mostly due to their mother. She's the nicest person that I've met so far." She asked why she wasn't here tonight. "She will be. Just not for dinner. She had a pack meeting that she couldn't miss, and everyone was all right with that."

"I have a lot to learn." She said that it'll be easier on her because she's not a pack bitch like she was. "You let them call you that?"

"I do. It's not so bad when they mean it the way that they do. I've had to hit the ground running, so to speak." She told her some of the things that were going on around town and how much she owed to Brew. "You'll meet him, too. He's a vampire who's ancient and has a mate. He and his friends are doing things around town to make it better, too. Like the greenhouse."

They talked about how many jobs the greenhouse was going to be bringing in and when it would be ready to see its first plants. Cass was brilliant and didn't treat her like she was someone who was new to all of the things going on around her. They had a lovely talk, and when they were ready to eat, she got to sit next to the woman and was delighted that dinner was so much fun. It was loud too.

After dinner, Conri, besotted with his wife,

told the group that they were going to have a baby. Mom apparently had been told yesterday, so it was now all right to share the news with everyone else. Congratulations were said all around, and they couldn't wait to see if she was going to have a boy or a girl. There hadn't been a girl born in their family for over four hundred years, and they were looking forward to it happening.

Going back to Kendrick's home, they all seemed to be all right with her living with him now instead of when they got to know one another better, they sat in the living room reading books. She'd found several on his bookshelves that she'd been meaning to read, and he was very generous with the couch for her to lie on. She could get used to this, she told herself, and was happy that he was seemingly such a nice guy. His mother said he was the greatest, but she said that about all her sons, so she wasn't sure how much stock to put into her words.

"Mom said to tell you that before you get a job, she might have something for you to do. It wouldn't take you out of the house every day, and you might hate it, but she has a charity that she works for that is in need of a couple more hands." She said that she was fine with whatever she got. "You might not want to say that to mom. She'll have you at every luncheon and affair that she can think of. Mom isn't now nor has she ever been a stay-at-home mom. And I think that's why we all love her so much."

"It must have been hard on her with the six of you growing up. And you said your dad was a bastard. She seems as nice as I've ever met, and I have a feeling that she can be a she-wolf when she needs to be." He told her about a time that Yuri had gotten in trouble at school. "My goodness, she didn't waste any time on going through the channels, did she. That's the kind of mom I want to be. And in answer to your earlier question, yes, someday I'd like to have children. But after we get to know one another a little bit more."

"Good. I'd like that as well." When she went up to bed around eleven, she waited on the side of her bed for Kendrick to come in, demanding that she have sex with him. Since he said he was coming right up after locking up the house, she was surprised and dismayed that it was midnight, and he didn't come barging into her room. Thinking herself stupid for even thinking that he'd do something like that, she huffed her way through her nighttime rituals and got into bed. What a day it had been for her, and she'd only known the man for four days. She was going to have to get her head on right, or he was going to have her committed. Sharon felt as off her noddle as she called her grannie sometimes.

Sleep wasn't long in coming to her. After getting

into bed, she felt her body relax a little at a time. When she reached over to turn off the light, she nearly dragged the glass of water off the side table with her. She had to relax again after that and found that she was much more tired than she'd thought that she was. Rolling to her side, she was asleep in minutes, but not before she thought of tomorrow.

They were going house hunting. She'd never done that before and was sort of excited to be doing it for the first time with Kendrick. He said that he moved around every few years so that he could get out of his head. She thought that, being around as long as he was, he'd be bored easily. But then she thought of all the changes that he'd seen and witnessed that she wished she could talk to him about that. It must have been scary and wonderful growing up when there was nothing but land around them.

Kendrick had told her that was how they'd adapted their last name. The three rivers had come together to form a 'y' in the city, and they had thought of it as a valley. Moving to the area that would later be known as Dresden, they had formed the little town with the new people when they started to arrive. Valley had become their last name for the city that they lived in. And what a beautiful valley it had been, he told her.

Dozing off a little with each breath she took, Sharon thought about her day. It seemed so long ago that she'd gotten fired, and it had only been a few hours ago. Kendrick had opened his doors for her and never once made her feel like she was going to be a burden on him. In fact, she'd never felt so welcomed as she did when he showed her around his house. Even when she'd been living with her grannie, she had never felt like she belonged. This home wasn't their forever home, he said, but they'd find one that would give them memories of their own to make.

Waking up once in the middle of the night, she didn't have any idea where she was. It took her several panic-filled moments to remember that she was at Kendrick's house and that she was safe. That was a new feeling for her, feeling safe. But after going to the bathroom and cleaning up after herself, she went to the window and looked out. She nearly screamed when she saw bright eyes looking up at her from the yard.

"Wolves." Almost as if whoever it was knew she was looking at him, he looked up at the window she was standing in front of. That was when she noticed that there were several more of the large creatures in the yard, and she watched as they seemed to be playing around. It had to be Kendrick and his brothers out for a night of running around. When she looked back at the wolf that had been looking at her, she was surprised to see him laying down on the grass.

She wondered what it would be like to become

an entirely different thing. She'd read books that were considered paranormal romance that would talk about how easy it would be to shift from human to wolf, then back again. She'd also read that they had to stay as one or the other for several minutes before they could shift back. Watching the other wolves as they danced around in the moonlight, she wondered again what it would be like to be able to not be yourself for a while. It must be exhilarating, she thought. Getting into bed when she realized that her feet were cold, she closed her eyes and went back to sleep. She knew she had a smile on her face; she could feel it there even as she closed her eyes.

Chapter 2

The next morning, he was at his office before Sharon came down for breakfast. On Fridays, he liked to get an early start on his day so that he could be out of the office by three. Usually, it was closer to five, but he did try. As the first of his patients was shown to their room, he had a feeling that today was going to be a longer day than he had anticipated. His first patient, Mr. Moss, set the tone for the rest of his day.

"What can I do for you, Mr. Moss?" Today, like all the other times he'd come in to see him, was going to be rough. "I've heard about Mrs. Watkins. I'm sorry that she passed. Have you found yourself another housekeeper yet?"

"No, and I damn well don't like looking. I don't know why you young people don't do more for the elderly. We're people too." He said that he knew that and thought about the elderly all the time. "Are you calling me old?"

"I am not. I was only commenting on your statement. Your ear looks better." He touched his fingers to the ear that had been infected a few days ago. "That cream must have really helped out."

"It did not. I had to resort to my own remedies. You quacks don't know a thing about the old-timey remedies that we had. It would do the trick, or you'd die from something as simple as a splinter." He knew that Mr. Moss knew that he was older than him, but didn't comment. It would get him backlash, and he didn't want that today. "When are you going to sell that house of yours? I'm thinking I need something bigger."

"I'm looking for houses right now. And my house has a lot of stairs. Weren't you just telling me that you hate the stairs in your current home? I would think you'd want something that is all on one level." He huffed at him, and he was all right with that. He thought the old man was lonely, and that's why he came to see him. But he was going to be on his best behavior today so as not to get him riled up. "Is your daughter still going out and fixing your pills for you for the week? You let me know if she's not. The pharmacy here in town will do them up for you for no extra charge."

"She does all right. She has to do something that makes her feel useful while she's still hanging around. I think she only does it because she's afraid of getting to the pearly gates and finding that she was a few good deeds short of getting inside. I got news for her. A few pills in a plastic container ain't going to get her inside either."

Mr. Moss was nearly ninety-four years old, and his daughter was in her mid-seventies. The two of them bickered and bitched at each other all the time. He didn't know what either of them would do if one or the other were to pass away. He knew it would be hard on the two of them. As much as they talked bad about each other, they loved one another just as much.

After seeing to Mr. Moss's needs, it was nearly noon. The man needed his prescriptions refilled, and in order to do that, he had to take blood samples. Since he was there, he told him that he was going to wait for the results, tying up a room for the rest of the morning. He didn't mind so much. Mr. Moss, for all his bickering about things, was a good man, and he seemed to have a soft spot for him.

The rest of the afternoon and into well after three o'clock, he worked on things for his patients and thought that he was doing a good job keeping them happy. The wait might be a little longer than normal because he liked to spend as much time with them as they needed. He thought that was why he never heard of his patients complaining about how long they had to wait. They knew that he'd give them the same service as he'd given the people before them. He loved his job as a general doctor.

At a little after five, he was headed home.

Mr. Moss had his renewals, and his blood work had come back fine. As fine as it could be for an elderly man anyway. After they left, his daughter was driving him to and from the appointments, he called to talk to Sharon.

"I'm fine. Are you off tomorrow? I thought that while I'm here by myself, I'd get us some appointments with a realtor. That way, she can show us what she has instead of us running around all over the place trying to find addresses." He thought that was a great idea. "Good. I'll get started on it right away. I'm not bored, but I need something to do to look forward to. I have a friend who says her husband takes her out to a restaurant when she sells a house. They can well afford it, but he always does that for her."

After getting off the phone, he decided to get some appointments that were for later in the week finished up early. Calling a couple of his patients, he was thrilled when they could come in today and have him get them finished up. He was on his last patient when he got a call from Conri.

"Don't freak out." He rolled his eyes and asked him why he'd say that to him. "I just got off the phone with the newspaper. They put an article in tomorrow's paper that another Valley man has been taken off the market. I didn't do it, and neither did Cass. I think someone who works at the paper did it thinking they had a good story."

"What does it say?" He read the entire article to him while he was standing in his office. "That's not so bad, I guess. Did they at least spell our names right? I'd hate to have to sue them for spelling something wrong."

"You're not mad." He said that he wasn't, but Sharon hadn't seen it yet; he didn't think. "I should have called her first. I never thought about her being at home and getting the paper. I only thought that one of your patients might get an early addition and spill the beans."

"No one has said anything to me. You might want to have Cass call Sharon. They seem to get along well." He asked him what he was doing. "I'm nearly finished for the day and was going to be heading home soon. It's really no big deal to me, but I don't know what Sharon is going to say when she finds out. We've only just met one another, and that might freak her out a little bit."

They talked about how it was coming out tomorrow and how he didn't care. He said that he'd talk to Sharon when he got home and would let him know how she felt about the article. Conri was a good brother for giving him a heads up, and he told him so.

"Cass said that she'd murder someone if they did that to her. Just so you know. I don't know that

I'd not help her. It's out there for people to read and speculate on, and now it's right up in your face." He said that he'd talk to Sharon about it and make sure that she was all right with things. "Tell her that I'm sorry that this is happening. Like you said, it's not that big of a deal to most, but to her, just being a part of the family and all, it might be something that she's not happy with. Let me know what she says."

"I will, I promise." Walking home, he wondered how he was going to tell her without getting her upset. The best way he figured was to just tell her. After that, they'd figure out what needs to be done, if anything. He thought about the ring that he'd had for her and decided that if she wasn't too upset with the way things were going, he'd offer it to her so she'd have something to show people about their supposed marriage. He was going to screw this up; he just knew it.

"Honey, I'm home." He could hear her laughter in another part of the house, so he didn't assume that she was laughing at him. As he hung up his keys by the door, he thought about how much he was already regretting moving again. He'd forgotten how much work was involved, but also knew that it was something that he needed to do. If not for him, then for Sharon so that she could start out new with her own home. She was on the phone when he got into the kitchen, where she was. After kissing her on the top of her head, he got himself something to drink.

While she spoke to the person on the other end of the line, he assumed it was the realtor that she'd been talking about. He asked his cook what they were having for dinner. She told him that Sharon had decided on burgers on the grill and asked if that was all right with him.

"Anything she wants." Nodding once, she went back to work on the potato salad she was making. He loved salads of any kind, but potato was his favorite. He usually ate it with chips crumbled up all over it for the extra crunch. He finally found himself a couple of oranges to eat to tide him over until dinner. It was still an hour away. When she got off the phone, she handed him a sheet of paper with addresses on it. "This is great. I didn't realize there were so many homes for sale in the area."

"She told me that a couple of them aren't even on the market yet, but will be soon. I'm going to take a guess that either someone has died in those houses or the market didn't do so well for them. She was very quiet about what happened to have them on the market after sitting empty for so long." She took a slice of his orange, and he smiled. "I heard from someone just before she called me, telling me that I'm married. Do you know anything about that? I think I would have remembered you asking me to marry you and saying yes."

He told her what Conri told him about it. "They don't know who did it, but it's safe to say that it was someone in the pack. They work all over the city in different capacities that help us out when necessary. Nothing illegal, but sometimes it helps to have papers filed rather than going through the steps of doing it the old-fashioned way. That's the way that Conri and Cass were married. Someone just put the paperwork in the right places, and they were finished with it. Would you like a large wedding?"

"No. I have no one who would be on my side." He said his family would be there for both sides. "I guess so. So there's nothing to worry about? You're not mad that the two of us are married now?"

"I have a ring that I made when I was younger. I have it on me now." He got down on his knees and smiled up at her. "Sharon Grace Taylor, will you marry me? I know we've sort of skipped a few steps, but I'm all right with that if you are."

"This is so sudden, don't you think? I mean, we've only known one another for about a week now. I'm all right with it if you are." He told her that she wasn't too romantic. "I don't know how to be romantic. No one has ever proposed to me before."

"And no one ever will so long as I have breath in my body." He slipped the ring on her finger and kissed her finger. "It fits you like you were there when I made it." She looked down at the ring, and he described how he'd made it. "I was just getting into gems and things when my mom suggested that I make some more simple things to sell. I started and stopped on this one so many times that I wasn't sure I'd ever get it right. Then Conri found his first wife—we never say her name if we don't have to—and I thought I was going to make something for my future wife when she came along. That was how I'd come up with that design."

The band was made of a wide piece of silver that he'd made too. There were little wolves in the design that he had fallen in love with when he'd put them on the soft metal. Once he got them just right, the ring sort of worked out on its own, so that he came up with the design that she was now wearing. He asked her if she liked it.

"I love it. It's just what I would have picked out for myself if I had the choice of any ring in the world." She held it above her head and looked up at it. "I love the wolves. I saw you the other night while you were out playing with your brothers."

"I wondered if you knew it was us. Rette called and said he needed a good run, so we decided to get together. We usually do it at night when there are fewer people around." She looked at him. "Do you really like it? We can get you something else if you want."

"No. This was made for me, and I intend to wear it for all time. It's perfect." He stood up and pulled her into his arms. "Are you going to kiss me now? I think that would be terribly romantic. I'm beginning to fall for you, Kendrick Valley. And when I do, it will be forever. So I hope you're right in saying that you'll never lie to me. I'd hate to have my heart broken after all of this."

"I promise that I will love you for all time. And I do too. Love you, I mean." She looked up at him when he lifted her chin up. "I'd like that kiss now if you don't mind. As you said, it would be the perfect way to start out our lives together."

She came into his embrace, and he pulled her tightly to his body. Brushing his lips over hers once, he was rewarded with her tongue coming out and licking them moist. Kissing her the second time, he deepened the kiss to the point of wanting her, but he never pushed her too far. She was beginning to trust him, and he wasn't going to put her on guard again for a single kiss. They had all the time in the world, and he was going to earn her trust if it was the last thing he did in his life.

~*~

"Whatcha reading?" Rachel said the hometown paper where she'd grown up. "Why do you care what goes on there when you have this beautiful town that we live in?"

David walked away, and she continued to read the paper. He hated that she loved to read, and when she started a book, Rachel would read the last chapter before starting on the book so that she'd know the ending first. So she was reading the paper the same way. Starting at the back and making her way to the front. It was the best way to work up to the news on the front page if you asked her. Not that it was ever all that much to deal with.

As she skimmed through the paper, she thought of her daughter. It was the first time she'd thought of Sharon since she'd moved here all those years ago. She'd be in her mid-twenties about now, she thought. Just old enough to be getting married on her own. As she got to the middle two pages, she skimmed lightly over the meals that would be going out on the senior meals this week, and then something caught her eye.

It wasn't as if she actually knew the Valley people. She knew who they were but didn't know which was which. She'd always thought that it would be wonderful to be married to one of them; the money alone would have allowed her to put up with a lot of things. But they'd been handsome and witty. Something her ex-husband, Richard, had never been. He didn't have two pennies to rub together most of the time. She hated being broke almost as much as she hated him. One of the Valley men had gotten married.

Having to go to the first page to read the beginning of the article, she was pissed that they'd not put it all on one page. So that she could read it all at once. But the front page had a blurred picture of the man and one of the woman with her name underneath of it. Picking up her glasses to make sure she was reading it right, she couldn't believe she saw her daughter's name as the bride. Calling for David, she had him read the name to her three times until she was satisfied that it really was her daughter.

"It says right there that her name is Sharon Grace Taylor. I didn't know you had a daughter old enough to be getting married. You said you were a single mom, and I just figured it was a kid out there someplace." She thanked him. "I don't know why you're thanking me. I always thought you were older than you said."

"Prick. I do have a daughter, and she's getting married to money." Not that she'd be able to get any of it. She lived clear out here in California, and her daughter lived in Ohio. It was a shame, really, that that much space separated them. She would really have liked to have seen her. "I have to call Richard and let him know. He'll be so pissed off. I don't know why, but I have a feeling that he'll be there with his hand out."

"Won't you?" She thought about it and then

shook her head. "I don't believe you. I've even heard of the Valley men. They're shifters and are as old as dirt. I'd have my hand out wanting a piece of whatever she's getting."

"I don't want any of it. Let her have a good life." And she knew she believed that too. She had a good life out here and wasn't going to go to Sharon after all this time, thinking or saying that she owed her something. She more than likely thought that she owed her the way that she'd left her with her mother. Rachel then wondered about her mother and wondered if, by chance, she was still around too. Picking up the phone after reading the entire article, she called Richard. Of course, his latest woman thing answered the phone.

"Why do you not carry it around like you're supposed to do? It's a mobile phone for Christ's sake. You're supposed to have it on you all the time." He said that all those who called him were bill collectors anyway. "I just wanted you to know that Sharon is getting married."

"Who? I don't know anyone by that name, and if they say differently, I'll have them sued. Why would I care if she's getting married in the first place?" She explained that it was their daughter. "I thought her name was Rachel or something."

"No, that's my name, you moron. I'm Rachel, and her name is Sharon Grace Taylor. Have you been drinking again? That's the only way that I'll believe that you've forgotten our daughter's name after all this time." He told her that it had been too long. "I would say that's what she'd say too if we were to show up and tell her we're still around. I just wanted you to know. She's marrying into the Val — " She stopped, and he asked her what she was going to say. "The Valeria family. Do you remember them?"

"No. Might if I was to see their face, I might be able to place them, but I'm terrible with names." She had a feeling that if he knew that their daughter was marrying into the Valley family, he'd be on the next plane to her. And she didn't want that from him for her. "Is that all you wanted? To tell me some brat we had long ago is getting married? If she thinks I'm paying for a wedding for her, she's going to be shit out of luck. I can't afford my rent, much less whatever is going on with her."

"That's all I called for." She shouldn't have called. Shouldn't have wasted her breath on telling him anything. She knew that now. Embarrassed a little that she might have steered him toward her daughter's happiness, she decided to call the one number that she had for her. And it was so old that she wondered if it would even work after all these years. Realizing that she'd missed something that he said, she put the phone back to her ear. "I'm sorry. What did you say?"

"I said you remember those Valley men? All them shifters that never aged a minute? They still hanging around down there?" She told him that she had no way of knowing. "I don't even know how you got the information on Rachel, much less anything that goes on down around there. If she were to be marrying one of them, I'd be there in a heartbeat. Now there is a reason to crash a wedding. Don't you think?"

"I don't know. I have to go. I just wanted to tell you about Sharon, not Rachel. How can you not remember that? Anyway, I have to get off here. I have things that I have to do." He said she was being strange. "Strange or not, I have things to do today, and only thought of you when I saw that Sharon was getting married. Or she is married. I don't remember now." She needed to get off the phone, and now he wanted to be talkative. She'd mess up somehow, and that would be the end of it for her daughter.

"What's going on? You never could lie. It's why I hated to be around you so much. You couldn't lie your way out of a wet paper bag." She huffed rather than say anything. Biting her lower lip, she decided that she should have her head examined for what she was doing. "Sharon, what the hell is going on?"

"Nothing, you moron. I've told you already that her name is Sharon, not Rachel. I'm Rachel. I wish I'd never called you." He said that he wished that as well and hung up on her. She was so relieved that she had to sit with her head between her knees and breathe before she could get up and have another cup of coffee. Things were going all right now, if he didn't get a burr up his ass and try to find out what she'd been lying about. Richard was right, she couldn't lie. When they would get caught without rent, she couldn't tell the landlord that it was coming in the next couple of days, when she had no idea if they were going to have it at all. She hated that about herself. Picking up her phone after getting a cup of coffee to fortify her, she called the only number that she had for Sharon and her mother. The phone was answered on the first ring, and she wasn't sure what to say.

"Hello, Mother. It's been a long time." Rachel burst into tears then. To hear her not cursing at her after all this time was a miracle. Not that she ever did, but it was something about her tone that had her babbling about her father. "I don't understand what you mean. Why, after all this time, would he want to have anything to do with me?"

"You're marrying the Valley family. Do they still have lots of money? That will bring your father to you faster than anything. The thought of getting free money from you would have him there soon." She asked if she was coming. "I can't. I don't have the funds either, but I don't know that I would. It's been too long for us to be mommy and daughter, don't you think? I was wondering about my mom. Did she pass away?"

"No, she's in Cedar Hill Nursing Home. She's not all there when I go to see her, but she's still alive. She'll be eighty-five in a couple of weeks. I was going to have cake with her. Not that she'd remember me, but she loves the fuss that I put up for her." She could hear the love for her mother in her voice, and it made her feel good. "Now, tell me why you think that Father would come to see me after all this time. It can't be because I've gotten married. I've been living without the two of you longer than you were around me when I was a child."

"He'll be there for the money that he thinks he can get from you. And even if you don't have any plans of giving it to him, he's going to think that he deserves it simply because he's your sire." She told her everything, even about how she read a book's last chapter before reading the first page. "I only meant to tell him and see if he'd be proud of you like I was. Then I remembered who I was talking to and wished I hadn't. I'm so sorry for that. I should have remembered what a gutless bastard he is."

"I don't understand why he'd care if I have money or not. It's not even mine but Kendricks." She told her that sounded like a good name. "Oh, he's wonderful. And a doctor. He works really hard all day and comes home to pamper me. We're looking for a new house to be our home to start our own memories."

As Sharon gushed on about her new husband, Rachel let the tears fall. She was happy and could feel it all the way across the states. When she began to wind down in telling her how happy she was, she asked her how long they'd been married.

"Only a few days. We just filled out the paperwork and had it filed. There was no point in having a wedding. I don't have any family around here, but Grannie, and she's not able to come. I should have invited you." She told her that it was all right, it would have brought her father to her sooner. "You think that he's coming? I don't have time for his bullshit. I'm not the kid I used to be."

"No, I'm sure that he's going to come to see you. Especially if he figures out that you're married to Kendrick. He sounds like such a lovely man. I hope you have plenty of years together." She knew that he was older than her daughter. By a great deal if the rumors about his family were true. She could see her daughter having lots of children by the man, too, and her heart did a little twist. "I'm sorry I left you the way that I did. I should never have married your father. He was a bastard and a thief, and I shouldn't have been anywhere near him when he got caught."

"Is that why you left me? That you were in jail?" Rachel told her how she'd spent the better part of ten years in prison for grand theft and other charges that had gotten them in trouble. Richard had spent fifteen years without any time off, like she'd done. "I didn't know that. I thought you just divorced and left me with Grannie because you couldn't decide on who was going to take me."

"No, we couldn't. And Grannie said she'd take good care of you. She did, didn't she?" She told her that she had a good life with her. "I'm sorry about that. I didn't know she hadn't told you where we were. It must have been for the best, however. You seemed to have grown up just fine."

"I had a job up until a few days ago, but since I live with Kendrick now, it's a long trip to work. So I've been doing things with his mom and family." She was jealous of his family getting to spend time with her daughter, but it was entirely her fault, and she wasn't going to be crying over spilled milk after all this time. "I don't know anything about you. I mean, are you well? Have you remarried? Is there anything that I can do for you?"

"No, nothing. It does my heart good that you are so happy. I've not been married again, but I do live with a man by the name of David Ross. He's a good man. Has a good job. We don't have a lot, but we're happy." She looked up at David when he came into the room with her, and he winked at her. "He wonders why I read the newspaper from where I grew up. I'll have to tell him with good reason now. I got to know you a little bit."

They talked a bit more, and Sharon said she was going to start calling her once a week until they were all caught up. Rachel said she'd like that, and when she hung up the phone, she sat on the chair and cried for a while. She really did sound happy, and she was glad that she'd called to warn her about her father. Now all she had to do was to make sure that she didn't let it slip to Richard that she was working on a relationship with their daughter. He'd want to be a part of it. She only wished that she hadn't called him at all, but then she wouldn't have gotten to talk to her daughter, and that was the highlight of her life. Her little girl had grown up without her around, and it was all her fault.

Chapter 3

After telling Kendrick about who she had talked to today, he asked her if she wanted to bring her out for a few days. She had to think hard on that and told him no, not yet. She might have to be dealing with her father. Then she told him what her mother had said about him.

"I looked up their trial. I had no idea that they'd gone to prison like they had. Grannie never mentioned it, and I never asked. All this time, I assumed that they just didn't want me and had left me with her." Kendrick told her that it would have been hard on her. "It was. For a lot of years, I was scared to make friends because I didn't know if they'd reject me or not. Not that my parents being in prison all that time is bad, I guess but it sounds like it didn't do my father much in the way of good. He's still getting into trouble with the law."

"Do you think he'll come here and try to get money from us? He won't if he does that. I want you to know that I've been telling people no for a long time, and this won't be any different just because I'm related to him by marriage." She told him she had not thought about the relationship he'd have with her parents. "I'm just saying that if he comes here demanding money, he's not going to get any. I know how to be a bastard, too, when it comes to telling people no when they want something that I have."

"I don't know what sort of person he is. My mother, either, for that matter. She seemed happy and good, but after all this time, it's hard for me to wrap my head around the fact that she called me. Just because she was worried about my father coming around." He told her that it could be just that. "I know, but I have to learn to trust her again, I guess. As I said, I know nothing about her other than what she shared with me on the phone. Not that I don't believe her, but I'm worried all the same."

"If he comes, we'll deal with him. If not, then that's fine too." She agreed with him. "How was your day, other than a mystery call from your mother? I'm assuming that you got things done with my mom."

"She's wonderful. Yes, I got things worked out with her and the job that she has for me. I don't know why she'd think I'd be any good at calling people for donations, but I'm willing to give it a try." He told her that his mom had a good feeling about her, and that was good. "I hope so. I'd really hate to disappoint her. She's a wonderful person, and I like her a great deal."

"She loves you, too. She told me that with you

and Cass in the family, she has women to talk to. I never realized that having six boys around all the time would be hard on her. But I'm thinking that it's been harder than I can even think. I think that my mom is wonderful too." They talked about the charity things that she was going to be working on with his mother before dinner. As they sat down to have their meal of roast beef and mashed potatoes, she told him how much she was looking forward to going house hunting in the morning. "I've set up appointments with the realtor and have things set up for us. I know that it's going to be a busy day tomorrow, but I think it will be fun as well. We'll just have to play it by ear on what we want in a house. I'm leaving that up to you on what sort of things you want in a house."

"Why me?" He told her that he wanted her to be happy. "I am. I don't believe that I've ever been this happy in my entire life. Just being with you has given me a better outlook on life that I don't believe that I've ever had before. It's like I'm awake for the first time in a very long time. I love that feeling."

"I'm glad that I could help." He laughed when she did, but he wasn't kidding. He'd fallen in love with his beautiful mate and couldn't have been happier with the feeling he had for her. All he wanted now was for her to love him as much as he loved her. And for the rest of his life, he'd be as happy a man as there ever was. "I love you, Sharon Valley. And I couldn't be a happier man than if you were to tell me that you love me."

"I'm falling in some way for you. I don't know whether it's love or not." He smiled at her, a little hurt that she couldn't say the words. But she'd get there of that, he was confident. "Do you suppose my father will come here?"

"I don't know him any more than you do. I can't imagine that he has the money. He might try to get that from you as well." She said that she didn't know how he'd get in touch with her. "If he knows where you live and your name, it wouldn't be hard to find you. Especially since it's been in the paper that we're married. We have contacts all over the world, so it would be difficult to say what newspapers have picked it up and run it."

"Mother gets the newspaper from here delivered to her daily. I didn't know that you could do that. Not that it matters." He said that it didn't. "I guess we'll have to wait and see what he does. I'm all for ignoring it, but I don't think he's going to just go away. From the way she talked about him, he's not a nice person unless he wants something. At least I can be on my guard when he gets here, if he does."

"He'll come. I have an idea that he's not going to let this go." She said that she didn't either, and they sat on the couch together. "I'd love to be able to just shut the world out, but I don't think that's going to be possible. But worrying about it isn't going to do us any good. We'll just be prepared for him when he gets here and deal with him as we need to. I'm not above making him disappear forever if he tries to harm you in any way."

"Thank you for that." She looked up at him as they sat there. "We're a boring couple, don't you think? I mean, we go to work, come home and eat, watch a little television, then go to bed. You'd think we'd have plenty to do once we got off work."

"I'm willing to do anything you wish; however, at the end of the day, just hanging out with you is about all I can handle for one man." They both laughed, and he smiled at her. "You're beautiful. I don't say that to you often enough. You're simply the most beautiful creature in the world to me."

"I needed that." She kissed him on the chin and then settled down on the couch. "I don't mind the boring part of our life. I have a feeling that it's going to get shaken up pretty soon, and we need to be prepared for it."

For the rest of the evening, they read their books. She'd found a couple in his library that she wanted to read, and with all the time in the world now, she was able to get through them fast. She almost hated to have them end; she was enjoying them so much. Sharon wondered if she could find more like that, but decided to wait until they moved. Then she'd have to find herself a good place to read in the new house where she could enjoy the comforts of home without leaving her little nook.

By the time bedtime was rolling around, she was ready for bed. It had been a really long day, and she just wanted to sleep until tomorrow. They were going to have fun in the morning, and she couldn't wait to see what was in store with them for their new home. She had a feeling that they were going to find it tomorrow and couldn't wait to tell her mom about it when she spoke to her next. This might not be so bad, having a long-distance relationship with her mom after all these years.

Getting ready for bed, she was nearly asleep when she realized that she needed to set her alarm. Pulling her phone to her, she got it set for seven since they were leaving at eight and rolled to her side to go to sleep. It was going to be a long day tomorrow, and she was excited to get a start on it. That and finding a house were high on her list of things to do.

Waking when the alarm went off, she was smiling when she got out of bed. There was a note on her side table from Kendrick, and she picked it up to read it. He'd gotten called in the middle of the night and would be home before they were set to go. She hated that he had to go out, but was glad that he'd let her know.

After taking a shower and getting dressed, she made her way to the kitchen. There she found not just Kendrick but his brothers, Lamar and Rette, as well. They had some paintings with them that they'd done and wanted her opinion on them. She clapped her hands and said she'd gladly tell them.

"Don't be too harsh. We're tender and shy about our work." She was shown the first one and fell in love with it. "We have an art show in a month and were wondering if these are going to be too much with it being close to fall?" Then she was shown the companion of the first one.

"I love them both. Did you both paint one of them each?" Lamar said that was it exactly and that they'd not even been in the same part of the studio when they'd done it. "I guess the saying is true about twins, you have some kind of psychic power. These are beautiful."

They were the same tree that she'd seen on their land when she'd visited them. Once she was able to get that out of the way, she could see that they'd each painted the tree with a different view of it. But the overall feeling of the painting was the same, like they'd been painted by the same person, or she thought they'd been in the same room and compared them as they went. Sitting them side by side, she couldn't believe how wonderful they'd been painted and was glad that they'd told her that if they didn't sell, she could have them.

"We're headed out to go house hunting in about fifteen minutes. Did you want to hang out with us?" Sharon told them that it could be fun, but they declined. They both had deadlines to hit and wanted to get caught up before they got to the last minute. "If you change your mind, just reach out to me, and we'll tell you where we are."

"Sounds good." After they left, taking their paintings with them, she sat down and had a quick meal, asking Kendrick about his work.

"I thought that I was going to have to deliver a baby, but turns out that she wasn't in labor at all. She still has about three months to go yet." Sharon asked if that was normal. "For a first-time mom, usually. They don't know what labor feels like, so they worry that they might wait too long to get to the hospital before the baby is born. I sent her home on bed rest for a few days, and we'll see if everything is all right. I did have her notify her OBGYN to make sure that he was all right with what I said and that she was to take it easy. I hope she does. It's going to be hard when the baby comes, and she's already stressing about it."

"I have a feeling that I'm going to stress out, too. I know nothing about babies or when they're kids. I've never once babysat in my life." He thought that was funny. "It's not. I wouldn't even know how to change a diaper if my life depended on it. You'd have to come home from work and do it for me."

"After a while, it becomes second nature. The things that you think you won't be doing will be something that you can't believe you do when your second one comes along. After that, then they nearly raise themselves." Now that she thought was funny. "You'd be amazed at how much I pick up from being around all kinds of mothers. Though I don't have any children of my own, I could pick out a layette and put one together without any trouble. I also know what will be needed and what isn't too. I hear a lot for someone who is only in the room for a little while."

"I'm glad one of us will know. I worry that I'll leave the baby somewhere and won't remember where I left it." He said he'd be there for her. "Good. See, I knew you were going to be useful when it came to having children. I'm going to be a mess just so you know."

"We'll get it there together." She thought of Cass having a child and knew that she'd be a pro at it in no time. "She would be. And having the pack around, too, for us will make it so that we don't have to look for sitters all that often. The elders of the pack will gladly do it for the chance to hold onto the Alpha's family."

"I sometimes forget that he'd the Alpha. I just think of him as Conri, and Cass is just my friend." He said they were that as well. "I know. I like them both very much."

After having a cup of tea, they made their way out into the city. There were six houses that they were going to be looking at, and she was excited to see what sort of offers they could make on them. That was something else that she'd never done, and that was to make an offer on a house. She hoped that Kendrick knew what he was doing, or they'd pay too much, she thought.

~*~

Kendrick didn't know why the house bothered him so much, but he didn't care for it. It was a house that had been added onto several times, and the stairs were just too much, he thought. It would go up a flight, then level out before picking up in another part of the house. Getting to the bedrooms would be a nightmare.

"I think that it's too weird." He and Sharon had exchanged blood before leaving the house so that they could talk without anyone knowing. He was enjoying her comments so far and was glad that he'd thought of it. *"Why are there so many stairs? Did they get a discount on them or something?"* Yes, he was enjoying the banter.

*"I'm near the woman now. I'll tell her that we're
headed to the next house so that we can move on. I don't like
the house either. Like you said, too many stairs that lead to
nowhere."* As he told the realtor that they were ready to
see the next house, she smiled at them. Like she knew
they weren't going to buy the place. *"The second house,
she said, is better because it only has one flight of stairs that
we'll have to figure out."*

The second house was a great deal better,
but the yard was a mess. It had dead trees that lined
the driveway. He didn't mind a little extra work on
something, but he didn't want to spend his life's
fortune in replanting a hundred trees so that he could
get rid of the ones that had died some time ago. Plus,
any of the flowers that had been planted to make the
yard look better had been neglected, and they were
mostly dead as well.

While there was only one set of stairs in the
house, it led to the second floor, where there were nine
bedrooms and two bathrooms. That, too, could be fixed,
but again it would be costly. He didn't want to spend
that much on a house that he only wanted because it
was time to move. Kendrick and Sharon drove to the
next house with no hopes of finding a house for them.

The third and fourth houses were fixer-uppers.
He didn't want that, and he was sure that Sharon
didn't either by her comments about having a house

livable by Christmas. That was still some months away, but if they were to take on a project house right now, there was no way that it was going to be ready by next Christmas. There was just too much work to be done on both of them that they'd make a single good house. That was sad when they had to think in terms of getting into a place to live by Christmas and knew that they had a slim chance of doing so.

The fifth house was nearly perfect. It did need some work, but not all that much. As they walked around the new home, he couldn't help but notice that there were no carpets in the place. Something that he was only just beginning to realize he didn't like in a home.

"They're not laid as yet so that the new homeowner can pick the colors out for themselves." He asked what would happen if they decided to go with hardwood flooring. "I would imagine that it would cost a bit more, but I could ask. This house has only been on the market for a couple of days, and I've yet to be asked that question. Thanks." She walked away to make her call.

"What do you think of this house?" He could tell she liked it by the way she squeezed his hand. "She's asking about hardwood floors over carpet. How do you feel about that? I should have asked you before."

"If your feet are cold, then put on some slippers.

I love the clean lines of the hardwood floor in the dining room. I didn't think I would, but it's nice, isn't it?" He said that was what he thought as well. "It'll take them about a month to get it taken care of, but I'd like to see the other house first anyway. They sell better when they have furniture in them anyway."

"I love the office. It'll be perfect for you to take for yourself. I can see myself using the library as my office. I don't need one, but it will be good to have one for the paperwork to get done that your mother gives me." She loved working for his mom, and it showed. "She said that all I'd need is a phone and a calendar, but I might need to make copies of something too."

The realtor came back. "He wants to know if you mean all the bedrooms or just the master? It won't be anything more if you go that way. However, he did say that the price would increase if you wanted them all done." He looked at Sharon, and she turned to answer the realtor.

"Tell him that we'd want the master for sure and at least two of the other bedrooms. That will be five that will need carpet." He only just realized that the house had eight bedrooms. It was a bigger house than the one they were currently living in. "Also, we'll need the kitchen repainted. I don't care for the darkness that's in there."

He hadn't either and was glad that she

mentioned it. The room was already dark with only the one window and door, but with the dark blue cabinets and walls, it seemed like a closet rather than a room they'd spend time in eating the first meal of the day.

While the realtor was on the phone, they decided to put an offer in on the house with the things that were to be done to it. Buying the lots on either side of them and the one in the backyard, they had a pretty nice space in which to live. He was excited to start a new life with Sharon. He accepted the offer, and they had a new home. They didn't even bother with the last house as they were satisfied with the one that they'd gotten.

With the purchase out of the way, they decided to head home and renew their packing. Mostly, it would be stuff inside of things. Like books and clothing. But none of the furniture. They were planning to start fresh, and this would be the only way that he wanted to do this. As they were sitting down to dinner, his brother Yuri came to visit. He had some investments that he wanted him to look into, and wanted to see about getting together for some investment information.

"We'll be halfway through the year soon, and I want to go over some of the investments that I think we should drop. There are only two, but they're not performing well, and there doesn't seem to be anything more we can do for them." He told him that he trusted him to do the right thing. "All right. I have two other investments that only you and I share, and I think we should double our money on. I can see a huge return in about ten years, and that's what we need to be looking at. You have a lot of other items in your portfolio that look good, too. We could sit down and go over them together, so you know where your money is going. I don't want you to think that I've ever cheated you."

"Christ, I know you won't do that." He hugged his brother. "I have all the faith in the world in you doing me right. But I'd love to get together and see what sort of investments you think we should work on together. I know that Conri has a couple that he takes care of on his own. I like doing that. It's like my own little nest egg."

"You've built up a nice nest egg for the two of you, too. Sharon needs to understand what she has in being mated to you." She said she'd like that as well. "Good. We'll have dinner one night and then go over money. Also, the property that you own has been transferred to Sharon's name, and in a few years, I'll make sure to switch it back. Some companies aren't so open-minded when the same person's name has been on the dotted line for centuries. There is a lot of property that I've fixed that way for you."

"So I'm a wealthy woman." Yuri, not one for understanding jokes, said that she was anyway with her being on Kendrick's books. "But I own all the property now. What if I were to leave Kendrick and take it all?" She was joking, but Yuri didn't get it.

"I'd hunt you down and make sure you understood that without my brother, you'd be nothing. I take care of what is mine." She told him that she had only been kidding around and would never leave Kendrick. That she'd fallen in love with him. "I'm sorry. I don't understand people. I hope I didn't offend you."

"No. I'm glad to know that Kendrick has someone in his corner. That's good to know, too, that you take money very seriously." He said it was the only thing that he took more seriously than life. "I love that about you."

"Did you just say that you love me?" Kendrick pulled Sharon into his arms for an embrace. "Say it again. Say that you love me. I want to relish in the fact that you've finally said the words I've been waiting to hear for a long time."

"I've fallen in love with you. It just happened." She reached up and kissed him on the chin, a place that he was beginning to find sexy. "I think it's when you turned to look at me when the realtor asked about carpet. It made me feel a part of the process that we're going through. Then it hit me. I'm your wife, and you love me. I should love you back, and I realized then that I did. I really did."

"Then I'm going to claim you. Right here and right now, so that nothing happens to you while we're still in the beginning stages of our life together." She asked him what that meant. "That you belong to me and that I belong to you. It'll make you immortal as well. We can live a long and happy life together."

"Then by all means do it." She sat down when he stood up. "Do I need to say it back to you to make the promise true? I don't want to mess this up with us when we're just beginning in our lives together."

"Yes, you do say it back to me. Sharon Taylor Valley, I pronounce on this day that you are my mate, and I give you all that I have from this day forward. Standing here in front of a witness, I proclaim you as my mate." She asked what she said to him in return. "The same. My middle name isn't important, but you have to mean it, or it won't give you any magic that I can share with you. And any magic that you have, and you do have a bit, you'll share with me."

"Good. Kendrick Charles Valley, I pronounce on this day that you are my mate, and I give you all that I have from this day forward. That would include my love for you. Standing here in front of a witness, I proclaim you as my mate." She looked up at him and smiled. "If you don't kiss me right now, I'm going to be very upset with you." How could he not kiss her when she really wanted it?

Pulling her into his arms, he lifted her chin up. She wasn't as tall as most of the women he knew, but he loved that her head fit under his chin. Brushing his lips over hers, he did that twice before her tongue came out between her lips and moistened them. He wanted that taste and took her mouth with his own. It was more than he could have hoped for this time as well.

He could taste the honey that she'd had in her tea at dinnertime. The taste of the chocolate scone that she'd eaten too. Pulling her in closer to deepen the kiss, her body molded to his like they were meant to be. Then he remembered his brother was there and pulled back slowly.

"I wondered if you'd remember me or not." He said it was difficult, but if he wanted to leave, that would be just fine with them. "I'm not leaving just yet. You'll just have to cool your jets, as they say. I really do want to get this cleaned up with you so I can get my end-of-year report to all of you on time. You know how I am about deadlines."

"I do know." Reluctantly, he pulled away from Sharon—who seemed to be just as shaken up as he was, but not before having to adjust himself. Sharon's face was as red as his when his brother laughed. "So what do you need from me about these investments that I have that you can't wait?"

There turned out to be several, and even though Yuri had them all lined up in order of need, it still took them nearly three hours to get them taken care of. He'd not realized how complicated his brother's job was in keeping them all in money for the rest of their lives. The next time he had an investment that he wanted Yuri to look at, he was going to have a bit more information for him, rather than just the name and address of a place. He was going to do his own research from now on, too. It wasn't a burden he was putting on his brother, he told him, but it might save him time in the long run.

By the time they were finished with the files, he was ready for bed. Kendrick had never been one for a lot of numbers. He could add and subtract well, but looking at future percentages that he might make on something wasn't what he did for a living. He was going to pay more attention to that as well.

Chapter 4

Richard waited on hold with the post office in his hometown to tell him who the Valeria family was. She said that she couldn't remember their name but would look it up for him. He'd been on hold for the past ten minutes and was starting to get aggravated. She was the post office worker; didn't she know everyone in town? Finally, she came back on the line, and he was ready to blast her when she laughed. Damned woman.

"I found the article in the newspaper. It's not Valeria like you were told, but Valley. Your daughter married Kendrick Valley. I guess about a week ago now." He asked if the paper said where they lived. "It doesn't, but I know they've been house hunting. They're using my sister-in-law as their realtor. She does a good job, too."

"Now this Valley person?" She told him again his name was Kendrick. "I don't care about his first name. But he's one of those rich boys, ain't he? One of them shifter things that lives out by the Smith estate?"

"They're very generous with the town and their money. I don't know that there are any other ones around." He was already plotting to get to Ohio. "I do know that they didn't have a big wedding. Just the justice of the peace married them off, and now they're house hunting. She's a good girl, that Sharon. I've seen her in here a few — "

He simply hung up on her. He had all the information that he needed, and that was that his daughter was rich. And by extension, so was he. Rubbing his hands together, he looked around his place to see if he had anything to sell to get him a ticket to the house they were buying. He'd be living with them by the end of the week, of that he was sure.

There was nothing left, of course, and he didn't have any money. A one-way ticket would be expensive but well worth the cost when he was sitting pretty in the lap of luxury. Yes, siree, he was going to have it all, or by god he'd know the reason why. But he had to play this right. It was only he who knew what sort of plans he had, and he had a feeling that was why his wife had lied to him. He knew something was off about her, and now that he knew, he was going to make sure that she didn't get squat when it came time for him to have it all. And he would too. He was a man who got what he wanted.

The only thing that he'd gotten out of his stay in prison was how to get what he wanted. And he'd had no trouble with that from day one. He was never bothered by the guards when he had a deal going down, and for the most part, they left him alone. He was fine with that. Richard had things going on that they didn't need to know about. While he was sure that they did know some of the things that he was working on, they never bothered to take him to task. He wanted to think it was because they knew better, but he thought, too, that he was just too good at his job inside to get into much in the way of trouble.

He thought about calling her, but didn't know how to do that. Everyone had a cell phone now, and as far as he knew, there wasn't a place that you could get to those numbers. He knew that his wife had it — he refused to say that they were divorced until he said so — but he knew that she'd not give it to him even if he begged. Sometimes he hated that she was so far away. He'd like to slap her around right now to get what he wanted. Richard thought of something else.

If she had her number, she more than likely called her to tell her about him. That wouldn't do him any good, so he would have to change himself around to be like someone that she could trust. He thought about how he was to go about that, and it went against everything that he could imagine. But that was the only way that it would work, so he had to go with that, or he'd be out of all her money.

Richard tried to remember if he'd ever heard how much money the Valley's had. It had to be in the millions right about now. Or even in the billions. He wanted that kind of money for himself, but he'd have to play his cards right. She'd not just want to turn it over to him, and he was sure that she'd have to have some convincing. He wasn't above knocking her around to get what he wanted, but he was going to try to con her into thinking he was a great guy. He could do it too.

Now all he had to do was figure out a way to get to her and her money. Or his money, as he was thinking about from her. Laughing to himself, he had a smile on his face that he couldn't get rid of. Money, so much of it that he could do what he wanted whenever he wanted. He might even have to move in with her so she'd not be spending his money stupidly. That was for him to do; hers was to make it for him.

He looked around his place three times before he came up with something of value. It wasn't going to be enough for him to get to her; he only needed a one-way ticket, but it would get him to the airport. He didn't have a car, so he couldn't drive, even if he had his driver's license. He thought about stealing one, but that wouldn't work; he didn't know how to get to the money without getting lost about a thousand times. No, he'd fly, and that was the only way that he could figure out how it would work.

Going to the airport and stealing a ticket was the only thing that he could come up with. He'd like to have first class, but he'd take what he could get for now. As soon as he was rich, he was going to never travel anything but first class from now on. He'd even have limo service to cart him around wherever he wanted to go. Even if it was just to the grocery store.

"But I'll have servants to do that for me." Richard was going to have servants do everything for him from now on. He didn't care what it was either; someone was going to wipe his ass if he wanted them to, and that was the way things were going to go. "Damn, but I wish I had thought of this sooner. I would have had better plans to get to her."

Of course, he didn't know how that would work since he'd not known anything about her. She was his daughter in name only, but that didn't matter to him. She was going to do what he wanted, or he was going to have to knock her around a bit. Or a lot, it didn't matter so long as he got what he wanted.

Richard didn't know what to do about her husband. He was a wolf, if he remembered correctly. And they were mean bastards. He'd have to catch him off guard or something. He wasn't above killing him. Then he'd not have to worry about how he'd inherit the money if what's her name got out of hand. He could see himself set up in their fine house for the rest of his life.

"I just have to figure out a way to get to her,

damn it." He had no idea how to get to the airport other than to tell some driver that he needed to get there. He'd never had the occasion to fly anywhere and thought that he'd be really good as a flyer. Maybe he'd get himself a jet so that he'd not have to wait in line at the airport. "That's what I'm going to do too. Just get me something that I can go around the world in all by myself."

He was going to have to spend his money better if he planned on it lasting until he died. Maybe he'd get the big wolf to change him into something like he was, and he'd live forever. That would be something to be able to be around forever. He'd have to make his money last, of course, but he could do that. As soon as he got the things that he wanted right off the bat, he'd be all right with waiting for the money to roll his way.

Packing himself a bag, he was out the door as soon as his driver pulled up. This was something that he could get used to, having his ass carted around all the time. Of course, someone would have to carry his bags; it was only fitting for a rich man as himself to have everything carted around for him. Laughing again, he told the driver that he wanted to go to the airport, and he was off. He was glad that he'd not asked him which one. He'd have no idea how to know which one of them would get him a ticket back to his home state.

Thinking he'd try and get his daughter's

number from his wife, he tried to remember what her name was. It was either Sharon or Rachel, but he didn't know which. In his phone, it only said 'wife' like that was supposed to help him. As soon as he got to the airport, he realized that things were going to be a lot harder than he thought. The only way he was going to get to Ohio was to read every one of the flights going out to see where he'd end up.

The closest airport to Dresden was Columbus, and he knew that to be a far drive. He was going to end up stealing a wallet, as it was so that he'd have walking-around money when he got to the place. Plus, he'd need food for when he got on the plane. The ride couldn't be any longer than a couple of hours at most, he figured, so he knew he'd not get anything to eat on this trip. That was another thing he was going to do. Make sure he had a meal on every trip he took in the event that he might get hungry on the way. Damn, but his life was going to be great. He nearly couldn't contain himself; he was so excited to get to his new life.

He found a family trying to wrangle about seventy kids. They really only had four, but that was enough for them to be distracted. The woman had a nice-sized purse that she wasn't paying all that much attention to, and he watched for his moment. He'd not take the whole purse, that could get him into trouble, and he'd only just started out. But he'd take her wallet that was sticking right out of the top of the thing like it was begging to be picked.

When she left to take one of the kids to the bathroom to be cleaned up, he watched the husband. He was nearly like every man he'd met that wasn't on top of things, just as distracted as the woman had been. As soon as he was turned with his back to her purse, he walked by, picked it right out of her handbag, and continued walking. It wasn't until he got to the bathroom himself that he looked and saw what his prize had netted him.

"Fifty lousy dollars." There were plenty of credit cards in the thing, but hardly any cash. He even looked at the tickets that were in the wallet and saw that they were headed to Florida. With all them kids, he figured they were on their way to the park down there to have a good time. Taking out one of the credit cards, he made his way to the counter to see if he could get a ticket.

The best way to get to use a credit card was to use it fast. That way, they'd have no idea that it had been stolen as yet, and you could usually get away with it. What he'd not counted on and should have been aware of was that the counter he'd gone to didn't have any outbound trips to Ohio, and he had to make his way down the wall of counters. It wasn't until he was nearly with his back to the people that he'd found one headed where he wanted to go. Ohio, here he came.

He was pissed off that there were no first-class seats on the plane he was using. He'd wanted to start his life out with the things that he was going to get for the rest of his days. But he figured that he'd have it all sooner or later, and this was only a little glitch in the system of him being a wealthy man. He'd get it all back and then some when he got to his daughter's house. He was going to have to figure out her name before getting there, or he'd blow his cover of him being a very distraught daddy who'd been away from his little girl for so long.

Laughing as he sat waiting on his flight, he was pleased as punch that he'd been able to get himself a ticket so easily. Now all he had to do was figure out a way to get from Columbus to Dresden, and he'd be there. The flight was going to be a nice short hop from here to there, and he thought about taking himself a little nap. Things were going just too well for him, and he knew it was because he'd been planning it so well. There was nothing to it, he told himself. Just get the money that he needed, and he'd be on his way. It couldn't have worked out better.

As soon as he was boarded on the plane, he found his seat easily enough. Since he'd not checked his bag, he didn't have to wait on the other end to get his things. Not that he had all that much. Just a few clothes and some pictures that he thought were his oldest child. Richard had four kids that he didn't have anything to do with—they didn't have shit that he wanted—nor did he pay any child support to them. They were on their own, was how he saw it.

He was landing in Columbus before he knew it and was on his way to his kingdom. By the time dinner rolled around, he expected to be at his kid's house eating dinner. If not, then he was going to have to figure out a place to stay until he got to their home. His home had a better sound to it, and he was looking forward to seeing his daughter more than he ever had in his life.

"Brats all of them." He looked over at the woman who had huffed at him. "Yeah, that's what I said, all kids are brats. No matter how you raise them, you've been the one who screwed up all along, and they're going to tell everyone they know about it."

"I'm betting that you weren't in their lives all that much either." He said he'd been in prison most of her life. That shut her up. "I'm a good man. I had nothing to do with her over the years, and look how she turned out. Rich as they come and going to support me for the rest of my life. I think that makes me the best dad in the world."

"You would." He laughed. Since he wasn't in a position to pound the woman, he just laughed at her. It made him feel good when she turned her back on him and didn't speak to him anymore. This was the way to fly on a plane. Make them uncomfortable so that they don't want to have anything to do with you anymore. That's the ticket, as his grannie used to say.

Now all he needed to do was to figure out a way to contact his daughter so that she could come and get him from the airport. Or all of this would have been for nothing. He'd be stuck at the airport for the rest of his life, and then what would happen to him? But he had faith in someone helping him out, even if they didn't know it. He'd find him another credit card with some cash this time and get there even if he had to hitchhike his way there.

~*~

Kendrick saw his last patient of the day and was ready for home. It had been a long day, made longer when he'd had to send two of his patients to the hospital for tests that were necessary for them to be diagnosed properly.

While he didn't usually bother the hospital about tests being done, he could do most of them in his office, and the time for them to be read would be quicker. And for the elderly man named Mr. Sherman, he wanted the results back as quickly as he could get them. The man was in his late seventies and seemed to be losing weight too quickly. Not a good sign at all for anything that might be going wrong with him.

The other was for another elderly person, but a woman this time. She told him she'd been sick with flu-like symptoms for a month now and wasn't getting any better. Like the man, he could have done the tests in his office, but they would be read by a professional instead of someone who only reads tests once in a while. He'd like to think that he was perfect, but he knew better than that. No one was perfect, not even Conri. Just as he was going over his files for the day, his office phone rang. Since it was a landline, he didn't bother answering it so that the ladies up front at the desk could take care of it. Almost as soon as he was ready to go to the next file, Gail came back to tell him he had a phone call.

"Hello, this is Doctor Valley. How may I help you?" There was some static on the line, and he waited until it was gone before speaking again. The person on the other end was shouting something about being picked up, and he didn't know what was going on. "Hello?"

"This is Richard Taylor. One of you married my daughter." He knew this call was coming or something like it. "I'm stuck here at the airport because you didn't send anyone to come and get me. Now they want me to move on, and I don't have a car yet."

"I'm assuming that you're talking about your

daughter, Sharon Valley?" He said that was it. Not Rachel. "No, I don't know a Rachel. Unless you're talking about my mother-in-law. She called today to warn my wife about you coming around."

"Warn you? I don't get why she'd even know I was coming around here." There was more shouting, and he came back on the line. "Look, you didn't send me a car, and now I'm considered trespassing."

"Had I known you were coming, I wouldn't have sent you one anyway. Although I figured you'd be showing up at some point. Why are you trespassing? People can usually sit in an airport for days without anyone bothering them. Or did you try something that got you into trouble?" He said that he didn't have a way to Dresden. "And like I said, I'm not going to provide you with one either. You got yourself this far; it wouldn't be anything at all for you to get yourself to us on your own."

"I'm trying to be a nice guy here, and you're not helping me at all. I want to see my daughter again. It's been a long time, and well, I miss her." He told him that it was a nice try. "What do you mean? I do miss her."

"I'm sure you don't, but let's not get into that. I don't know how you figured out this number, but I'm not going to be sending you a car. Money, either if that was your next question. As I said, you've gotten yourself this far; you should be able to get yourself the rest of the way here. If not, then that's good too." He asked him why he was being a bastard. "I'm not. I'm a man who plans on protecting his wife when or if you show up. This way, I have some control over when you arrive. Or if not, like I said. You seem like a resourceful man. You do what you need, and hopefully you'll be caught at something, and that will be the end of the visit to our home."

"I suppose Sharon is there with my daughter." He corrected the name. "Whatever the hell her name is. I suppose my wife has her head up her ass so far that you can't tell them apart."

"Rachel declined to come out. Said that she didn't have the funds, and when I offered them to her, she said she'd come out when they got to know one another better." He asked why he didn't offer them to him. "Because you're thinking of coming here for a handout, and I'm not going to be giving you anything. I've been around for a good long time and have learned that when people like you come around, the best way to deal with them is to say no from the very start. I'm really good at repeating myself on that, too. You're not going to get anything from us when or if you get here."

"I'm coming by god, and you damned well will hand over what I want. Or I'll be making trouble for you." Kendrick just laughed and said nothing. "Laugh it up, wolf boy. When I get there, we'll see which one of us comes out on top. I'm a man that gets what he wants, and you have something that I want. Money. And I'm going to have my fair share of it, or you'll pay."

"I'm not afraid of you, Richard. Or should I call you Dick? I like that better anyway. I heard that you can't stand that shortened form of your name." He said his name was Richard and not Dick. "I don't care. Come on and try me. I've been around longer than you and know just how to hide bodies when they get in my way."

He was sputtering when he hung up the phone. Reaching out to his brothers, he let them know that Dick was calling numbers of the Valley men and looking for someone to help him get to Sharon. He also told them how much he hated his new nickname.

"Did he say what he wanted? How the hell did he get this far in only one day?" He told him how he'd been marked as trespassing at the airport and was asked to leave. *"He must have been caught at something or close to it for them to do that. I'm assuming that he wants money. Isn't that what Rachel said he'd be coming for?"*

"Yes, it's money. He told me that he was going to get it, and I was going to hand it over to him. I'd like to see him try that." Conri asked how he'd gotten to the airport. *"I never thought to ask. No doubt he would have told me*

and blamed me for — he's pissed off that I didn't have a car sitting there waiting for him when he arrived. I, like you, never dreamed that he'd get this far after only one day. I wonder who he had to rob to get a ticket here? I'm sure that's what he did. Stole someone's credit card to get a ticket."

"Maybe that's what he did to get himself in trouble at the airport. He either got away with it once and was counting on the second time to come through, or he got caught nearly stealing a wallet off someone, and they put up a fuss. That's probably more like it. They found that he didn't have any money on him, and no one was waiting to bring him here, and he got caught." Kendrick had to agree. *"You don't have to worry about any of us helping him. But I do appreciate you giving us the heads up. But I have a feeling that he's going to be coming here by hell or high water sooner rather than later. He'll have some story, no doubt, that will have someone feeling sorry for him, and they'll bring the bastard here because they felt sorry for him. Just our luck, some nice people will be conned out of something to help the bastard."*

After closing the connection to his family, he called home to talk to Sharon. Telling her that her father was at the airport didn't surprise her as much as it did him. She'd been talking to her mother again about her father, and she said that he had an iron will that would get him what he wanted. Well, he was going to be shit out of luck when it came to getting money when he got to their home. He was better at a lot of things than Dick was when it came to telling people no.

"I'm worried that he'll hurt someone to get here. Like steal a car or something." He said that he'd been trespassed at the airport, so they'd be keeping an eye on him until he was gone from the area. "From what Mother said, it would be just like him to steal from someone and mess up their vacation plans. I wonder who he stole the money from to get from his place to Columbus."

"I never thought to ask. I'm sure by the time I hung up on him, he would have been just pissed off enough to tell me anything. He said that it was our fault he was in trouble at the airport because we didn't have a car waiting for him. Also, he thinks your name is Rachel. I doubt if he cares enough to figure out your real name before he gets here." She asked if he thought he'd get here. "Yes. He's gotten to Columbus already. It'll be nothing for him to get to you the rest of the way. Just be careful when you go out and remember what I told you. You're immortal now; he can't hurt you."

"He can't hurt you either, right?" He said that it was right that they were both safe from him harming them, as was his entire family. "I hate that he's gotten this far. I was hoping he'd be too stupid to try and get to me after all this time."

"When there's money involved, people will go to great lengths to get what they want. Or what they deserve. I have a feeling that he's going to think that just because you have money, and you do, then by extension, he has it as well. I've no doubt that he's going to get himself into big trouble when he gets here." She asked if she'd hand over the money. "No. Not for any reason."

"He might try to take me and hold me for ransom. What would you do then?" He told her. "Just like that? You'd kill him?"

"That'll be the only way to deal with him, is to kill him. Because paying him for you would take everything I have, and I'd not care, but he'll never stop. He'll be coming back again and again for more until there's nothing left, and blame that on us as well." Sharon said that she loved him. "And I love you so much. Nothing will happen so long as we stick together. You stick close to me, and nothing will get through me to get to you."

"I'm so glad to hear that." He said it was the truth. "I'm glad too that we've got the pack at our backs. Conri said they'd die for me simply because of who you are to him. I don't want anyone dying for me, but I'm glad to know that they'll protect me at all costs."

After he got off the phone with her, he told his brothers that Sharon knew what was going on. Conri said he'd send more patrols out to keep the house safe.

He'd put nothing past the man. Thanking his brother, Conri repeated what he'd said to Sharon. The pack would die for her, and that was the way that it should be.

Chapter 5

Richard wasn't happy. He wasn't even a little pissed off, but so powerfully angry that his head hurt. Rubbing his forehead while he tried to talk someone into taking him home, he thought for sure that people were more of a bastard than they used to be. Back before he'd been to prison, he'd have been able to bum a fiver off of someone for a call or two. Now, everyone was keeping their money around where he couldn't get to it. No more free handouts for him today.

It didn't help that the airport police were watching his every move. All he had to do was get out of the airport, and he'd be just fine with them. But he couldn't get a ride if he was hanging around the door like a homeless man. Damn it, but he just wanted to get to his money and fuck the rest of them.

Talking to that person on the phone, he couldn't remember his name, he'd been hung up on, and that hadn't gone over well. He'd broken the phone when he'd slammed it into the receiver. The police were pissed off about that, too, but since they knew that he didn't have any money, they'd let it slide. All he'd done was brush up against someone, and they'd yelled that he was trying to take their wallet. He'd almost had it, too, but for the screaming.

He'd seen the man in line at the coffee shop. He'd had a fistful of money that would have choked a horse. Noticing where he'd kept it, inside the jacket pocket, he nearly had it out when the man went crazy, saying that he was stealing from him. Of course, the police didn't believe him, a man with nothing but twelve dollars in his wallet that he'd stolen in New York. So they'd been following him around since then in pairs. Like he was going to be able to get home with them tagging around him all the time.

Then he just started begging people for a ride to Dresden or something close so that he could get home to his daughter's wedding. That's what he'd been telling them since he started out, and so far, he'd had no takers. People were just too untrusting, is all it was, and he didn't know how to overcome that. His first plan of action when he got the money was to come back here and flip it around in everyone's face who dared disbelieve him when he'd told them that his daughter was wealthy and that she'd make sure that he was all right from now on.

The first thing he was going to do after killing her supposed husband was to make sure that he never had less than a thousand dollars in his pockets at all times. And he was going to carry them around in twenties, so he could tell people to keep the change. He'd only do that to people who had treated him poorly, and so far, that was just about every person in the fucking airport that he'd come in contact with.

But in order to do any of that, he had to get to Dresden and figure out how the hell that was going to happen, which was costing him all his patience. He looked over at the cops who were still following him around like they had nothing better to do.

"Will one of you call my daughter up and tell her where I am?" The first guy said no, but the second guy said he'd do it. "She's got a husband as a doctor, so you know I'm good for the call."

"I don't care if her husband is a homeless man. The less I have to follow you around and your sad attempts at getting home, the better off I'll be. What's the number?" He didn't know it. "What do you expect me to do? Dial every Valley in the phone book? That's not going to work."

"I called the doctor, and he said he was her husband. That's all I remember because we got disconnected somehow." Sure, he did, and his mother was a saint, he thought. The fucker had hung up on him, is what happened, and he wasn't going to let that slide either. "There are a bunch of them in that little town. They all have the same last name. I don't know that they're all in the phone book, but the doctor is."

Just as he was making some headway in getting her on the phone, some guy walked up to them and smiled. It wasn't one that he'd be friendly with, but he found himself smiling back.

"Are you the guy who's heading to Dresden? I'm headed to Zanesville, and I can make it so I go through Dresden on my way home." He asked him if he knew the Valley men. "Everyone knows the Valley men. You'd have to be stupid not to. I can take you as far as the main drag, then I'm headed home. Won't be too far out of my way."

"I'll take it." He was ready to get there when the cop found the number. There was a service on when he called, so he left a message. "Tell them that I've got a ride and I'll be there in a couple of hours. They'd better be waiting dinner on me because I'm powerfully hungry."

He thought about other things he could say to them, but there were too many people around. What he had to say to them was private like and something that would get him into trouble with the people around him if he were to let go that they didn't want him there. He was coming by god, and they'd better be ready for him. Richard was about as pissed off as he'd ever been in his life after this, and they were going to pay for it.

He'd not realized how late it was when he got into the man's car. He had a woman with him who was fat and ugly, but he told him that she was going to have a baby and had come home to meet his family. Whatever. He just wanted to be in Dresden, where he could take his shoes off and be comfortable. He'd already walked more miles today than he had in a couple of years. His feet were burning to be set free.

Richard didn't know what to do with himself in the car with the couple. He was sleepy, that was for sure, and found himself dozing off once in a while to the quiet rumble of the road beneath him. As soon as he got comfortable, he made sure that he had his bag close at hand, he curled up into a ball, and closed his eyes. They were driving, and he had no reason to make sure that they knew where they were going.

"We're here." He nearly cursed at the man for waking him up. "Hey, mister. We're here. It's time to wake up."

He got out of the car and stretched. There was the main drag just like he remembered it, with cars in the yards and pizza joints all over the place. Of course, he couldn't see much, not with it being as dark as it was, but he knew that come morning, everything would come back to him and he'd be able to find his daughter. Right now, all he wanted was a good meal and a bed to lie down in.

"You need anything?" he said that he could use a cup of coffee, but he'd get it on his own. "I wasn't offering to pay for anything. I just meant, did you get your things out of the back of the car? We need to be going."

"Yeah, sure. I've got my bag. You really came through for me, and I appreciate that. Thanks." He was trying out his being nice thing when he realized that the kid and his wife were driving away. "Good riddance, too, to you. I've got better things to do than fawn over you and your fat wife."

Huffing his way to the convenience store, Richard wondered why there wasn't a car for him. He'd told the service that he was going to be here, and this time, there would be no excuses for him not to have a limo just waiting to pick him up. That's the least they could have done after the way that they treated him at the airport. As he walked into the store, he saw that they were about as dead as he'd been on his feet. Richard decided to chat it up a bit to figure out where they lived so he'd not be out on the street all night.

"Hiya. I'm looking for the doctor here in town. Valley is his name." The woman behind the counter said that he was closed at this time of night. "I know that, I guess. I was wondering how one got in touch with him if he had an emergency or something. I'm his father-in-law, Richard Taylor."

"You're related to Sharon?" He had to keep telling himself that was her name. Not Rachel, like he kept thinking it was. He told the woman that she was his daughter. "We heard about you. You abandoned her when she was just a kid because you had to go to prison. Yeah, we heard all about you, Dick."

"It's Richard, not Dick. I told him that when I was speaking to him. We had a slight misunderstanding, and I'm here to see him. Do you suppose you could call him and tell him that I'm here waiting to be picked up?" He was trying his best not to get upset right now. All he needed was for the police to be called, and him being put in jail, too. For all he knew, they'd not bail him out either. "I just wanted to make sure they know that I'm in town and have no place to go. So I need to get in touch with him."

"Can't help you with that. We're not to even tell you where he lives. You made it clear to him that you were only coming here for money, and he's not one to give it up so easily." He was starting to get mad, and he was sure that the two women knew it. "Now you find yourself a nice place to hunker down and see about getting some sleep. Not that I think you're going to have a better day tomorrow. You'll find that the entire town isn't too keen on helping you out. Not after the way you treated that lovely daughter of yours."

"I got caught, that's all. Had I not been caught, then I'd of not gone to prison. So it's not my fault. Besides, she was with my wife's mother all this time. It's not like I left her on the streets to survive on her own, now did I?" Neither one of them looked convinced, and he rubbed his hand over his face in frustration. "Now see here. He's my relative, too, now. I demand that you call him up and let him know that I'm here. He'll have to sort out what you're doing to me later. I'm tired and hungry and want to go to bed."

"You don't want to see your daughter first? Geez, Mister, I would have been bouncing around trying to see her more than my son-in-law. He's a good man, too, but so is your daughter in the event that you didn't know that. She's been helping me get my checks to the post office so my kids can't take them anymore. I suppose you'd be out there taking them from me if we were related." He said he didn't know what she was talking about. "My checks. Because of men like you taking from me, I don't get my check every month. But that daughter of yours, she's making sure that I get them at the post office so no one bothers me no more."

"That would just piss me off, and I'd take it from you later." He'd not meant to say that and regretted it as soon as it left his mouth. "Look, this has nothing to do with you finding my family. I just want you to call them for me and tell them that I'm here."

"Not going to happen. As I said, you should just find yourself a cardboard box to sleep in while you're here and then move on. We have no use for your kind of people around here. I liked it when you left the first time, Dick. That's what we called you in school. Dick the dick. I remember you now."

"I don't know what it is you're talking about." He did remember that name, but not the woman who said that he knew her. High school had been a blur of one kind of trouble to the next. He'd hated being around here, and right after he'd gotten out of prison, he'd made himself get as far away as he could. Never to return. But he had a good reason to now, and these people were going to help him. "If you knew me in high school, then you know what sort of person I am. Call my son-in-law up and tell him to get his ass down here before I start to cause him all kinds of trouble. I mean it too. I'm in no mood to be fucked with."

He should have known better. Almost as soon as the words left his mouth, two cruisers pulled up in front of the store with their lights on. Putting up his hands, he glared at the two women and told them they'd get theirs. He wasn't above buying this place when he got his money and firing them both. Stupid cunts.

Richard was taken to jail, but not before he had to sit in the back of the cruiser, which was parked in the parking lot with their lights on for an hour. He knew it was an hour too because he could see the big clock in the store proclaiming that it was well after midnight when he got arrested. The whole town was going to pay for this, he thought. Just as soon as he found his daughter and that husband of hers, they were going to pay too. This was just ridiculous. He'd told them he was coming; everything should have been ready for him.

He supposed in a way it had been. The police certainly knew who he was and where he'd been coming from. Even the two women in the store seemed to know a great deal about him coming. Well, everyone was going to pay for this as soon as he had his money. There was no point in his pussyfooting around anymore. He was going to get the money, or he'd know the reason why, damn it. They will know better than to mess with him next time. Richard was going to be as ready for them as they'd been ready for him. And they weren't going to like it any better than he had.

~*~

Kendrick had been notified as soon as Dick got out of the car in Dresden. He'd been dropped off right in front of his house, and he thought it was funny that he'd not even known that. When he got to the convenience store, he'd been notified once again that he'd shown up there. It was just like clockwork the way the town was keeping tabs on the man. He loved every second of it.

The fact that he'd been arrested was funny to him, too. He'd never get his address unless he gave it to him, and that was going to cost the man. Sharon was worried that he'd hurt someone, and he was as well. But for now, he was safe and sound in the jail system and not bothering anyone around. Teddy, one of the officers at the jail, said that Dick was powerfully upset with them as they'd arrested him for vagrancy.

Dick had had twelve dollars on him when he'd been arrested and claimed that he had family in town that was going to take him in. Kendrick had made it perfectly clear that not only was he not taking him in, but he didn't consider him to be family either. Now that he was off the streets for the night, he was going to go to bed and sleep peacefully.

"What have you found out?" He'd thought that Sharon had gone to bed and was startled by her voice in the darkness. He told her what he'd found out. "So he's back in jail where he belongs. Did I tell you that Mom said not to trust anything he says? Not that I have any plans of doing that, but it does worry me that you're being so cavalier about all this."

"I promise you that I'm taking this very seriously. He's going to be pissed off when we finally do talk to him, and I figured that he'd be more forthcoming about his plans when he is. I have already had Brew read his mind. He's going to try to act like you're his best thing since sliced bread and that he has missed you when he can't even remember your name." She said she was worried. "I am as well. He's a man used to getting his own way, and it's not going to happen around here. I know what I'm doing, but the smartest thing I'm doing is making sure I know where he is at any given moment. I promise you that he's not going to harm you."

"He'll try to take me so that you'll pay." He'd already told her that he'd be a dead man if that happened, so he didn't say anything this time. She knew, however. "I don't want you to have to kill him either. I won't feel bad that he's dead, but I will be upset that you had to do it. That he drove you to kill him. Don't you understand? I don't want it to come to the point where you end up killing him and going to jail for it. I've only just figured out that I love you and I like having you around."

"I'm going to be all right. If it makes you feel any better, I can have my brothers kill him if it comes to that. And it might not. But if he harms you or tries to take you, then all bets are off. He's a dead man." She came to him and wrapped her arms around his waist while putting her head on his chest. "I'm not going to be hurt either. I might break a nail, but that's about it. I promise you I'm taking this as seriously as I can."

"Who's Brew? You might have told me at one time, but right now I can't remember?" He explained that he was an old and powerful vampire who just so happens to be good friends with his family. They helped one another when they needed it, and Brew, being as old as he was, could read minds without any contact. It was one of his superpowers. "He's Calla's mate. He calls her his Calla Lily. I remember now. They're a nice couple. Scary but nice."

"He would love that you said that." Guiding her up to the bedroom, he had not realized it was so late. He told her that the house was being protected by the pack and everyone was watching the new house, too. "The flooring will be done in a week, then we can move into the rest of the house. I'm glad you had the idea to move into the other rooms so that we could get it set up. I do love the living room furniture that we picked out. It's comfy and sturdy."

"You're trying to distract me." He laughed, just simply threw back his head and laughed. It felt wonderful to be so free with his laughter as he was with her. "You do that well, laugh, I mean. It sounds really good and makes me want to join you. When this is all over, I want you to make me laugh daily. All right?"

"It would be my pleasure. I would love to hear you laughing like you mean it." He kissed her gently

on the mouth and opened her door. "Now go to sleep
before I have to get up in the morning. Remember
what I said, don't leave the house for any reason unless
someone is with you. He might be in jail for the night,
but I don't know when it is they'll release him. All
right?"

"Yes, all right. I understand. He's out there no
matter if he's on the streets or not." He kissed her again
and turned to his end of the floor to go to bed. "I want
to make love to you. Not tonight, I'm too stressed out,
but soon. Would that be all right with you?"

"It would be fantastic." He adjusted himself and
laughed again. "I might need to take a cold shower
before I head to bed tonight. You're all I think about
when I'm going to sleep."

Hurrying to his room before he embarrassed
himself again, he got in the door and closed it quietly
behind him. Leaning against the door, he closed his
eyes. It was that or sob. He wanted his mate with all
that he was, and the sooner she was ready, the better
off he'd be. But he'd never rush her. It was her body
and her time to choose when they made love. Going to
his bed, he decided that he would be all right tonight
without taking a cold shower and laid down. He was
nearly asleep when Conri contacted him.

"I'm assuming that you know he's in jail." He said
that he'd been informed as soon as he'd been arrested.

"He's not going to be easy to convince that he isn't going to get your money. I'd look for him to do something desperate when the time comes. He might even try to take Sharon away from you in order to make you pay."

"I've already told her that he'd be a dead man if he tried that. She doesn't want me to go to jail. I don't think anyone in town would care enough to put up a fuss, but then I've never killed anyone before. Do you suppose he'll go away nicely if I continue to tell him no?" Conri just laughed. *"Yeah, I didn't think that would work either. But I'm going to try to convince him that I'm not going to give in to blackmail or anything else he has in his mind right now. Brew told me that he was going to try to pretend to be nice for a while to lure us in. I wouldn't have thought that would have worked in the first place."*

"No, he's a man who is used to getting things done the way that he wants." He said that he figured as much. "I don't want you hurt either. I know you can't die, but the thought of either one of you, you or Sharon, getting hurt makes me scared for the two of you. I'm going to have extra pack around both your places until this is taken care of. Also, I'll have one on him at all times. He won't be able to take a shit without us knowing everything there is to know about it."

"Thanks for that. I know that the pack is willing to do what you want, but I'm going to have to think of a way to thank them for their extra work. It's not every day that I

have to have help, and you've no idea how much I appreciate it." He told him that would be nice of him. *"It's the least I can do. They're helping me out a great deal by doing this. And protecting Sharon is the best part. I've explained to her about going out and how she needed to be careful."*

"Good. I hate to say this to you, but you know she'd be stronger if you were to bond with her." He told him what she'd said tonight. *"I can understand that, too. Stress is a mood killer of all kinds of things. But the sooner the better. Especially since it doesn't look as if he's going away anytime too soon."*

That worried him too. That Dick was here to stay until he got himself killed or he ended up back in prison. It would suit him just fine either way, but for now, he was going to try his best to reason with the idiot. There was no way that he was going to give in to his demands for money. If he did, he'd be paying the man for the rest of his life, and that was going to be a long time.

Rolling to his side, he thought about how he had to work in the morning. It was only a few short hours before he should be getting up, but he did try to sleep some. But his mind couldn't shut down on the fact that he'd actually made it to town and that he had already caused trouble. If Dick kept this up, he might not have to lift a finger to get him out of their lives; he might well do that all on his own.

Getting up just as the alarm sounded, he was out of the shower and dressed quickly. He knew that Sharon would be up soon, so he hurried by her door so that he'd not be tempted to go in and wake her up. He really did need to get to work today, and watching her sleep wouldn't get him anywhere close to getting his day over with.

By the time he'd seen his first three patients, he was feeling the effects of not getting enough sleep. However, around noon, he started to get his second wind and was feeling better. Eating his lunch helped, as he'd not had any breakfast, but he was glad for the one that he'd gotten. A nice sub with chips was his favorite, and he enjoyed every last bite of it.

After lunch, he was sailing through his day on nothing. He yawned a few times when talking to patients, and he apologized several times for that. Kendrick was glad that they didn't have any plans for tonight, as he wasn't going to make it on how he was feeling. Dragging himself home, he sat down on the couch, sort of glad that he had the house to himself, and took a nap. He didn't think he'd move for a week the way he was feeling.

Waking up to the sound of the front door opening, he was shocked to see that it was just after seven. He'd slept for nearly three hours, and he felt better for it. He knew that he'd go to sleep as soon as he got into bed tonight and wasn't the least bit sorry that he'd taken such a long nap. He was glad to see that Sharon seemed to be in a great mood, too.

"I've spent the day with your mother. She and I got a lot done." He asked her what she'd been up to. "We've figured out the charity foundation money. She thought there was a bit of it missing, and all it was that someone had added the column up incorrectly. I was glad to be able to help with that."

"I'm sure Mom was glad for your help, too. Missing money is always something that would bother her. I'm glad the two of you are getting along so well." Sharon said that she was wonderful and easy to get along with. "I'm happy for the two of you. What did Cass have to say about today?"

"She had her own things going on today and couldn't meet with us. It was fun spending time with your mother all on our own like today, but I did miss Cass. She's fun to be around, and I learn so much from her when she's talking about the pack. I had no idea that dues were to be paid each year and that they go to the pantry for those who need it. I'm to understand that Conri has a very good pack of about four hundred wolves. That's a lot of people to be in charge of."

"He's been doing it since our father was killed by the pack. He's made it a very profitable pack, and people are staying. Which isn't always true of a larger pack. They get bored, or there aren't any jobs around, so they move on. Some families have been with this pack since it was formed. Generations after generations have stayed because Conri runs a good pack."

"I think that's wonderful." He said that he'd been a good man and that was why people stayed. "I think it's all the family that makes them stay. As I've been told numerous times, this family is good to the community, and it shows in everything that goes on around here."

After dinner, he kept napping. He wasn't ashamed of being so tired that he couldn't stay awake, but missed some of the conversation that Sharon was having with him. Finally, at nine-thirty, he made his way up to bed. Just as he was getting ready for sleep, he realized that he'd not heard from anyone about Dick.

Good. The less he heard, the better. Rolling over to his side to sleep, he was closing his eyes when something else occurred to him. He'd not set an alarm. Fuck it, he thought, he didn't have anything to get up for in the morning, and he was going to sleep until he was ready to wake up.

Chapter 6

Richard wasn't happy that he'd been arrested. He'd had money on him and thought that they were just doing this to piss him off. Well, he was taking names, and when he had his money, he was going to make sure that they understood that he was the one making the rules, and they were going to follow them.

He really was remembering names so that when he was in charge, he could make them pay. And pay they would. When he'd been in prison, he'd been so high up on the food chain that whenever he wanted something done, they didn't ask him how he wanted it to happen, but when he wanted it done. Now was going to be no different. And if his daughter thought that he was going to put up with her shit, then she'd better be rethinking her life choices. He was going to be in charge, and there wasn't shit she could do about it.

"Dick, you have a visitor. And since you've been put on cell watch, then you'll have to talk to them here." He asked what that meant. "When you threaten the officers here, you pay the price. Now they'll be down in a minute. I'm to warn you too that you're being recorded with both verbal as well as actions. So watch what you say or not. I don't really care."

He was another one who was going to pay for this bull shit. He didn't even understand why he was in jail when all he'd done was try to find where his daughter lived. No one was cooperating with him on the outside nor inside the jail, and that was going to change, too. He might even decide to run for mayor of this little town, and then they'd see who was in charge. He was, and there wasn't going to be shit that anyone could do about it. He looked up when a man and a woman stood in front of his cell.

"Am I supposed to be impressed that you're here? I don't know who you are, so get on with whatever you're going to say and get out. I have plans to make." The woman laughed and told him that she was Sharon Valley. "So? Is that supposed to mean something to me? Well, it doesn't."

"I'm your daughter, moron." He stood up and told her to come closer to the cell doors. "I don't think so. I like where I am right now. Out of your reach. What is it you think you're going to get by coming here and demanding to see me? Nothing as of right now." He said that he wanted her money. "No."

"What do you mean, no? I'm your father, and I should be able to order you around as much as you need to be. And if I think you need to have a pop to the head, then you'll take that too." She just stared at him without saying a word. But it was the smile on her face that pissed him off the most. "What do you have to say for yourself? You're to have respect for me and do what I tell you."

"I said no. I'm not going to give you any money, nor am I going to give you the opportunity to do anything to me. I'm a grown woman who has her own ways, and you're nothing to me." He said that he was her father. "Only because you were the sperm donor who created me. You're nothing to me."

When she turned to walk away, he told her to get back here. He looked at the man who was still standing there without saying a word. Asking him what he was looking at, he laughed a little.

"I'm imagining you in your casket with your throat ripped out. I'll do it too." He stepped closer to the bars, and Richard felt his cock shrink to nearly nothing. When he put his hand on the bar, and it morphed into a great paw, he laughed. It wasn't a humorous kind of laughter, but more like he was a little insane. "You so much as touch the ground that she has walked on, and I'll tear your throat out without a second thought. And no one would care at all that you're dead. Especially not Sharon."

Long after he left him standing there, Richard stood near the bars and thought of nothing. His mind was still on the fact that he really was a wolf and that he'd just threatened him. There was shit that he could do about it; he knew that the police would be on the other man's side, but it scared him not just a little that he'd be able to do what he said, and he'd be dead. Not just dead, but he had a feeling that he'd suffer badly too.

When his meal was brought to him, he was still standing at the bars. He didn't have any idea how long he'd been standing there, but his knees were cramping up, and his body felt like it had a rod up his spine. Sitting down on his cot, he didn't bother with complaining about his meal. He was just glad to have something else to focus on rather than the fact that all the rumors around the man were true. He really was a monster. And a badassed one too.

After his dinner tray was taken away, he still couldn't wrap his mind around the fact that he'd been threatened. Not that he didn't believe that the man would do as he said, but that he'd actually threatened him, of all people. And he'd gotten away with it, too. There was no doubt in his mind that the police wouldn't back him up if it came down to it. So he'd be fucked either way if he were to complain about it.

Every time he closed his eyes, he could see the paw while it was there. It wasn't a small one either, but a great paw like you'd see in the zoo or something.

And the fact that he'd only had to do it the one time to scare him also made him pissed off. Why would he care, he told himself, if the man could make himself into a wolf? He didn't, that's what.

The more he convinced himself that he had nothing to worry about, the more he thought about the paw. He just couldn't seem to get it out of his head that he'd been hearing all those talks about the man, and they turned out to be true. He had to wonder if the fact that he'd heard other rumors might be true, too, like the one that he could take your blood and read your mind. That was something that scared him more than the paw did. Richard liked having secrets.

Looking at his hand, he could see the marks on it. There were little places where there was blood, and he tried to remember if he'd taken any blood from the wounds. No, he kept telling himself. There was no way that he would have missed him doing that and put his hand down. He no longer wanted to look at the paw prints on his hand.

Closing his eyes again, he could see the paw and wondered if the rest of him as a wolf was big. He'd never seen a wolf up close before. Big dogs but never a wolf. Now here he was related to one, and there wasn't much he could do about it. Richard wondered too if his teeth were as big as he had imagined them to be. Shivering once, he sat up on the side of the bed and looked around the dark room. Everywhere he looked, he could see those shining eyes glaring back at him, and it made his chest hurt a bit. Christ, he'd been scared. He still was, but he'd admit that to no one but himself.

Getting up to go to the room's only source of light, he watched the clouds move over the moon. It was just a night like this that he'd been arrested and sent to prison. Dark and gloomy, the clouds darkening the sky. He sometimes thought about that night and wondered how he'd been caught. He'd been really good at covering his tracks.

He just knew it had been his wife who had turned him in. Fat lot of good it had done her if she'd been the one. She'd spent time in prison herself and hadn't gotten out any earlier than he had. Or had she? He didn't know precisely when she'd gotten out. They'd been in different prisons. He'd have to check into that as soon as he got someplace to look on a computer.

While he didn't much care for the machines, he knew that they had their usefulness. He'd use them, but only when he had no one around him to make fun of the way he one finger typed. Or that he had to rely on spell check in order for him to get a word right. His spelling was atrocious, and he knew it. But then he'd never graduated from high school, getting out when he'd been a freshman the second time.

His life had been hellish when he'd been a kid. His parents were both in the church so much that they were rarely home. He'd have to go at least several times a week to be a part of the church, but he didn't care for it. Just like other organizations, there were just too many rules that had to be followed in order not to get into trouble. He was forever in trouble when he was there.

Finally, his mother had taken him aside and told him that since he wasn't going to cooperate with the church, he'd been in trouble just that morning for questioning the pastor about the existence of god, he'd have to leave their home. No amount of trying to convince her would do any good either. So at seventeen, he was kicked to the curb with a hundred dollars and his clothing in a backpack. He'd never seen them again.

Then he'd met and married Rachel. He was sure that was her name because his daughter had said her name was Sharon. She'd been an all right person when he'd met her. Going to work every day meant that he had money to spend when he wanted it. Also, since she worked all day, he had her apartment to himself for most of the day, and that suited him just fine as well. Richard could get into all kinds of trouble during that time, and he usually got to knock her around, too, when she came home complaining about working all day and then having to clean up after him, too. He nipped that in the bud before it became too much of an issue.

Then one night during his robbery period, she'd been with him. Richard would always say that it was because of her being with him that got him caught. They'd been stealing a car that they really didn't need — it was just the joy of it for him when the police came out of nowhere and busted up their little fun. Of course, it wasn't just the car that they'd taken, but they'd robbed the house. He'd also tied up the homeowner and beat him up a bit, too. That made it so that he had a home invasion on his record, too.

He'd been surprised that Rachel had gotten any prison time at all. All she'd done was complain about getting caught. Then, when they got to the house, she refused to go inside with him, so he'd done all the other stuff on his own. He'd actually enjoyed beating the man and had been thinking about it a great deal since then.

If he'd been sure that there wasn't a cell phone on her when they'd gotten to the house, he was positive that she'd called the cops on him. It would have been just like her to do something like that. She was forever bitching about how he didn't have a real job, but he thought that robbing people of things that he wanted was hard work. She never understood that. Then there was the fact that she left him with their kid all day long while she worked.

She refused to take her with her, and that would piss him off. But every day, he had to keep an eye on the kid just to make sure that she wasn't hurt. By the time she was old enough to go to school, it got easier, but he still resented the fact that he had to make sure that she was healthy and unharmed when Rachel got home from work every day. And she'd check her out, too, just to make sure that there were no bruises on her.

While she could be a pussy about some things, she sure was a good momma in keeping him in check over the kid. He might well have enjoyed knocking her around a bit. She'd been an uppity sort of kid. Then, when they'd gone to prison, she'd made sure that someone would watch over her and picked her momma over his own. Not that he knew where she was or anything, but he was hurt that she'd never even asked about her.

Feeling better about going to sleep, he laid down on the cot and closed his eyes. He'd had fun in prison, but it wasn't a place that he wanted to go back to. Just too many rules were holding him back from having some real fun. Like none of the guards would allow him to touch their gun. That was just fucked up.

Also, he couldn't get in merchandise like he wanted, so that he could make some hard money. Too many rules is what he thought, and didn't understand why, with all the rules, someone didn't pass some kind of law about it. Laughing to himself, he couldn't believe the shit that would come up in his mind. If people could hear some of the shit that he thought of sometimes, he'd be in some kind of loony bin. Or a padded room for sure.

Finally able to get some sleep, he thought about tomorrow. He was going to have to figure out a way to get out of the mess he was in and get his daughter to turn over her money to him. He'd not harmed her as a kid, and that should get him something, he figured. Even if she didn't give it all to him, she should at least give him half of it. It's what he deserved after all the years that he'd had to put up with her bull shit.

~*~

Standing in his office, Kendrick popped his neck twice before he felt like he could face his patients. He'd been in a sour mood since he'd left the jail, and it wasn't getting any better. Just as he was set to go out and see his first patient of the day, his door opened, and there stood Sharon.

"Are you in a better mood?" He just growled at her. "Very mature. I know you understand how to use your words. But in the event you care about my opinion, I thought that yesterday went well. I got to tell him off, and you got to be all macho and take some of his blood. I thought for sure you'd be tormenting him about now, but here you are with your feelings hurt, acting like a child without any cookies."

"I'm not being childish." He realized how badly he sounded and growled again. "I'm not being childish. I'm pissed off because he thinks that you're stupid enough to just hand over the money without questioning him about it. You're not going to do that and never would. How would he begin to think that was ever going to happen?"

"I'm sure it's because he thinks that it's his way or nothing. And he's gotten used to that somehow, and now he thinks that the world owes him, and he can do just whatever he wants. Are you going to sulk all day?" He said that he wasn't sulking either. "Could have fooled me. You're really in a shitty mood, and I'm not. I wonder why that is."

"Because you can't see into his mind to see the things that he's done. Not to mention he's stupid. Did I tell you last night that he can barely read? That's the type of person that we're dealing with right now." She said she didn't care what his mentality was. "I do. I wonder if it was his upbringing."

"His father was a pastor at one time, and when Dick started acting out, they asked him to step down. About the time, he was being kicked out of school, too. He was a freshman at seventeen and not going to pass the grade for the third time." He asked her how she'd found that out. "Cass did one of those deep background checks on him and my mom. The only reason that she ended up in prison is that she was with him the night he was arrested. They claimed that she was driving the getaway car. I don't know how that was to work since he stole a car and was driving it when they caught him."

"Where were you when this went down?" She told him she'd never thought to ask. "More than likely in the car with one of them. They neither one sounds like they have much in the way of intelligence."

"Mom didn't graduate from high school either. The reason is that she got pregnant with me. Her parents kicked her out, or she might well have gone on to make something of herself. As it was, she and my dad got married so that she could put him on her insurance at her job. That's what Cass figured out. Because almost as if the ink had dried, he was on her insurance policy at work."

"Have you been talking to your mom?" She said other than that first time, no, she hadn't. "Why not? I thought you wanted to get to know her."

"I'm going to call her once in a while, but I have no feelings toward her. I don't remember her at all from when I was a child. And she did drop me off at my grannie's home without telling me why. Grannie didn't say either, but someone should have told me. I just thought that they didn't want me anymore."

"I want you. I love you." She smiled at him, and he felt better than he had all morning. "You're very sneaky on how you got me out of my bad mood. Thank you for that. I didn't know how I was going to see patients with this anger built up."

"There was no reason for you to be angry in the first place. He's in jail and will be there for a while. Also, did you know that he's threatened the police taking care of him? He's making a list of people that piss him off so that he can have them taken care of when he has all the money. Do you think he has any idea how much money there is?" Kendrick said he doubted that the amount means all that much to him; he just wants it because he doesn't have it. "True. I can see that. He's like a bully who wants all the toys on the play lot and gets pissy when he can't have them all. Yeah, I can see that being the way he thinks."

"Do you want to know how much money we have?" She shook her head and smiled at him. "Why not? I mean, there is a great deal of it to be had. I've done very well for myself — for us, I mean."

"I'm happy that I have a roof over my head and food in my belly. That I can go to the store and get what I want when I want it, so long as I don't go nuts." He told her she'd have to go really nuts to spend it all. "I won't do that. But you tell me that we're all right, and I believe you. Putting a number on it will just make me crazy, so that I have something else to worry about. Is it enough that I don't have to worry about it?"

"There's more than enough for you to not ever have to worry about it. I promise." She nodded and told him she was headed home. "Did you only come here to get me out of my mood? If so, I can't thank you enough."

"I came to chase you around the office, but I figured that wouldn't work out when I got here. You're really busy." He said that it was Monday. "I'll have to remember that from now on. I can't have any fun with you here at work on Mondays."

He was laughing when she left him there with a kiss to his chin. He was glad that she'd been able to get him out of his mood. It might well have hurt someone's feelings when they had to talk to him like he was. He was just stepping into the first patient's room when it occurred to him what she'd said. She wanted to chase him around the office. Did that mean…?

For the rest of the day, he was busy enough that he didn't get to think about what she meant. But when he did, he was thrilled that she'd come in and talked to him about it. Being chased around his office wouldn't work out all that well on any day of the week, as he'd taken the door off his office when he first started seeing people. He wanted there to never be a closed door when someone wanted to talk to him. Now he was beginning to regret that move.

By the time he was ready for a break, it was lunchtime. It was his turn to stay at the offices, just in case someone came in early to their after lunchtime appointment, but he didn't mind. He'd had his lunch brought to him in the form of a large salad with chicken on it and was content to sit in his office and eat it. When the others came back, he went to the bathroom and washed up before he was ready to begin his day again. Kendrick did love his job and was glad that he was enjoying it enough that he wasn't bored with it.

By three o'clock, he was ready to call it a day, but he still had about three hours to go. He'd gotten to tell one of his patients that they were going to have a baby and had been high on their happiness for the rest of the day. When his last patient came into the office, he was caught up enough that he didn't have to hurry through. He loved ending on a good note like that and was happy that he'd had such a productive day, too.

Driving home, he was happy to remember that the movers were going to be moving the few things that they decided to take from the house with them. The floors in the new house looked better than he thought they would, and he was glad that they'd had their bedroom have hardwood floors as well. He loved the golden sheen that was there when the sun hit it just right and thought that if the floor got cold, they'd just pull out some slippers. Yes, he was happy with the changes they'd made in the kitchen as well.

The cabinets and the walls had been painted a dark blue. It was so dark in the room that it was difficult to feel comfortable in it. Once the walls had been painted a bright while and the flooring a light color, he was happy to say that he thought it was perfect. With the countertops being white with blue swirls through it, he thought they had the most perfect kitchen ever built. He couldn't wait to have a couple of meals cooked in the thing.

He'd had staff at their first home and was glad that they all decided to come with them to the new one. He would have hired all new staff if not for Sharon loving them, and now he didn't have to have someone come out and train them. Things were going just as planned, and he couldn't wait until they were staying full-time at the new home.

The beds had been put together and made up just yesterday. All the rooms had been cleaned, and the carpets that were in the few rooms that they were in were vacuumed and ready to be used. All they needed to do was move in with their clothing, and things would be done. He'd never had such an easy move before. He thought maybe Sharon had been right and this was going to be their forever home. He loved the sound of that, too.

Forever meant something so much more than it had before Sharon had come into his life. He was thinking in terms of being together forever, like the fact that she was going to be by his side forever made him feel like life was worth living for him. As soon as he got to the new house, he was going to put down roots — like trees and plants that would be there for them forever, too. Kendrick was excited about everything going on today, all of a sudden, and was happy that Sharon was home when he got there. Picking her up and swinging her around, he kissed her on the mouth before setting her back down on the floor.

"Well, aren't you in a great mood. So much better than when you left." He said it was because of her. "Thank you for that. I needed a pick-me-up today."

"What's wrong?" She told him how she'd spoken to her mother today about her father, and she said that he should be in jail forever. "I agree, but without more information, that's not going to happen."

"He has no income, and he lives in a nice apartment that he pays for in cash every month. That's all she's told me about, but I agree with her. How is he supposed to be paying for this place without any income? He doesn't even get Social Security. He was denied that when he went to jail the first time for stealing checks and cashing them. It seems to me that he's back up to his old tricks."

"While I agree with you in that it sounds fishy, no one is going to put him in jail just because he's paying his rent on time. I'll have Cass look into it—" She said that she'd already spoken to her. "Good. One more thing I don't have to do. But if he is dealing underhandedly, then they're going to have to catch him in the act rather than just saying that he's up to something. Understand?"

"I do. I don't like it, but I understand." She pouted her lower lip, and he kissed it. "That was nice. Now all I have to do is figure out what he's doing so that I can catch him at it, so that he goes to prison for the rest of his life. That sounds easy, don't you think?"

"Not at all." She growled at him, and he had to laugh. It was such a wimpy growl that he couldn't help but think of her as a small puppy trying to do it. Not wanting to upset her more, he didn't mention it. "But you can bet that if there's something out there, Cass will find it. She's good at getting to the dirt on things."

For the rest of the evening, they talked about what he could be doing to get money all the time. They thought about everything from cashing checks again to running drugs, high-end things that would get him serving a lot of prison time. Since neither of them was a lawyer, they couldn't get past the few things that they'd seen on television, and that didn't give them much to go on. They'd just have to wait on Cass to see what she was able to unearth for them.

Chapter 7

Yanick hated working. He loved what he did; however, he didn't care for the people that he worked for, the staff that worked under him, nor the drive all the way to Columbus every evening that he had to go. Sitting in his car outside the restaurant, he closed his eyes and leaned his head back on the seat. He still had twenty-five minutes before he had to be inside, and he wasn't going to rush getting in there under threat of death. It was too much for him.

"I have a question for you." He smiled when Cass reached out for him. *"It's not a big deal that you might not know it, but you're the first person I thought of, and that's why I'm bugging you. Are you at work yet? I don't want to disturb you while you're carving up veggies or something."*

"I'm sitting in my car trying to convince myself to go inside to work. I don't actually carve up the veggies. I have people who do that for me. Should they do it wrong, then I get to be the bad guy and tell them to redo them. It's the highlight of my day to be the mean boss." She asked him if he really was a mean boss. *"No. And that's the reason that I dislike my job so much. Everyone thinks I'm a pushover, and I have no control over what happens in*

my own kitchen. What is it that I can do for you, my dear sister?"

"What do you know about prostitution?" He wasn't sure how to answer that, so he didn't. Which seemed to be fine with her as she clarified what she meant by asking him. *"I believe that Dick's girlfriend is running a prostitution ring out of his apartment. While none of the work goes on in the place, there is a lot of activity going on in and out of there. Women mostly with a couple of men. I think what happens is that they show up, get their assignments for the evening, and leave. The reason that I think that is because the neighbors complain about the amount of cars going in and out of their end of the complex. Nothing is going on inside the place other than the phone calls and the people going in and out. I think they might be turning over their cash too when that happens, but again, I can't be sure."*

"And why would you think that I'd have any idea what was going on with something like this? I'm flattered, don't get me wrong. I never would have thought of doing something like this in my wildest dreams, but tell me how you got to that conclusion." She told him. *"So you think that all single men know how this works? I think you're giving us a great deal more credit than we can ever hope to know. I, for one, never used a prostitute. And I doubt very much that anyone I know has either, including my brothers. But I love the way your mind works. Sure, I can see that happening. But unless you pointed it out to me, I would never have gone*

there. My mind isn't on where my sex comes from so much as I — never mind. I don't pay for sex."

"I think I might have bitten off more than I can chew with this one. I don't even know how I came to that. But it makes sense. Like when he has money, he has a great deal of it. I know this from talking to some of the people that he owes money to. And there are a lot of them. But when he's broke, he never seems to be worried about where his next buck will come from. He pays his rent in cash along with his other utilities. I can't find a credit card in either of their names. He doesn't drive, but she does, but she doesn't own a car. I think she uses services to get around. Him too, but I don't know who he uses. She's right out front with her money. Wears designer clothing, expensive shoes, and makeup. She also gets deliveries about three times a day." He asked her how she came to the conclusion of prostitution. "I don't know that either. It just popped into my head, and I couldn't get rid of it. I'm thinking of calling the police department and telling them what I've found out. However, if they think I'm nuts, then there will be that that I have to contend with."

"I don't know anything either, but if he's not there and she's doing it, he could just say that he didn't know, and that would be the end of his part in it. Unless you know that he's part of it too." She told him that she didn't, but he was right about him not being there. "He's suddenly has reservations in a hotel right now, he's supposed to stay in when he gets out of jail. Which might be sooner than* *expected. Do you suppose that she sent him money to live off of? And why steal a credit card or cash if she has so much of it? It's sounding more and more like he has nothing to do with the ring, and it's all on her. I mean, I don't know, but if you use your logic on it, it sounds like he's just some guy who lets his girlfriend do whatever she wants while he's away."*

It was time for him to go in, and he didn't want to. He was having too much fun speculating on things with Cass. As he made his way into the back door of the restaurant, he talked to her more about this supposed job that his girlfriend had.

"Even if you are right and it sounds like you've given this a great deal of thought, how would you get someone to go there and figure it out? Call it in? I would imagine that they have plenty to do in New York with this sort of thing." He put on his apron and looked at the night's specials. He was going to need a lot of carved-up veggies tonight and some steaks. He got the people working with him to get on that right away. *"This is the most fun I've had in a while. I wonder where your mind went when you thought this up, but I'm also not sure if I want to know. You have a very strange way of thinking of things."*

"That's why, because I think outside the box." He said that was good of her and laughed. People turned and looked at him, and he waved them off. *"This is really thinking right outside of the box, isn't it? I do wonder*

at times if I should have been a detective or something. I love looking for clues and getting to the bottom of things."

"Yes, but thinking about them and actually doing something about them is different. One will give you a headache, the other might well get you killed." She told him she was being careful, and he believed her. With her breeding, Conri would make sure she was being extra careful as well. He did wonder if his brother knew about what Cass was doing and decided that he wasn't going to say anything. He liked his head right where it was.

For the rest of the evening, the two of them talked about it off and on. It made his evening go better, and he wasn't in such a terrible mood when something went wrong. He knew it wouldn't be his fault when it did, but somehow it always came back to being his fault in some form or another. By the time he was ready to go home for the day, they'd decided to see if Conri could get another pack member to watch over the place and see if what they were talking about was true. It might not get as much jail time for Dick as they hoped, but it might also get him out of the way for a while. It was worth looking into.

While driving home, he thought about Dick and what he was doing to Sharon. He couldn't believe the greed of some people and was sorry that she had to go through all this. He'd experienced some greed when he'd taken a couple of different women out. They had it in their heads that since he had money, he should want to spend it on them. He did to a point, but not like they wanted and expected.

As he was getting on the highway to go home, he thought of his job and how much he hated doing it anymore. He used to love cooking, but now it was nothing more than another chore that he had to do. It was about time he changed his career and did something that he liked and couldn't for the life of him remember doing anything but cooking since he was old enough to reach the stove. What he needed to do was find himself a mate so that she could shake things up for him like the other two had done for his brothers.

Not that he was actively looking for a mate. But then neither had his brothers. They just appeared. But he was more on his toes than they'd been and thought that if she came along, he'd be more in tune with her than his brothers did like Kendrick. He seemed to not have any idea what he was doing most of the time, and he blamed that on not having sex with his partner. Or that could be just him. Yanick didn't know much about mates, but he did know that he wanted one in his life.

The last time he'd moved, he thought it was a house that he could live in for the rest of his life. It had everything that he needed in the way of places to use. It was larger than he thought that a couple starting out needed, but he thought that spare rooms were just that spare. He wasn't under any kind of obligation to fill them out with children. He didn't even know if he ever wanted little ones running around. He would like a mate that he could travel with and have fun with.

He knew, too, that if a mate came along, he was going to have to be in a better mood all the time. She might well make it so that he was, but worrying about his job wasn't going to set well with either of them if he didn't get himself into something that was better than he had right now. Yanick worried too much to let a job take over his life like this one was doing. He either needed to get over the little problems that were going on at the place daily or find himself a better job. The better job might not come, but he knew that he needed different more than he needed better. He was bored with cooking where he was.

Pulling into the gas station that was open when he went by it, he filled up his tank and decided that his personal tank needed filling as well. He'd eaten at the little restaurant before that the station had on its premises. The food wasn't fancy, but it was filling and good. Something that he'd make for himself if he were at home at the time.

Ordering breakfast, he was brought his tea and biscuits when his menu was taken away. The soft butter was good, and he enjoyed one of the warmed biscuits even as he was putting honey in his tea. He had just put his spoon down when someone sat down across from him. It was just a kid, so he didn't say anything at first.

"Don't tell him nothing." He wanted to correct the kid, but decided now wasn't the time. Almost as soon as the boy, he could see now, took off his jacket and hat, someone walked into the diner and looked around. "He's looking for me, but he won't find me if you play along. He thinks I'm a boy."

Well, that changed his mind, and when the girl pulled her hair back from her face, he could indeed see that it was a little girl. She must have been about ten years old, but since he'd not been around kids much in his life, he was only guessing. The man came to his table and asked him if he'd seen a little boy.

"Boy? No. I've just been sitting here with my daughter since we came in, and you're the first person I've seen since then." He nodded and moved to the next table. When his food was brought to him, the girl took his pancakes and started dressing them up for herself. When a glass of milk appeared, too, he had a feeling that he was being had somehow and was going to end up in jail before the night was over. "What's the deal? I just want to have something to eat that doesn't involve me going to prison for it."

"Margaret knows who I am. She covers for me

when I'm in trouble." He asked what sort of trouble she was in and how much was it going to cost him. "Just your pancakes. Margaret will take them off your bill when you're ready to leave. Chill your jets, why don't you? I'm not hurting you."

She wasn't, and he should have been relieved. But he wasn't. Just having her in the booth with him was making his wolf a little antsy, too. But since he was hungry and she wasn't causing him any grief, he ate his eggs and bacon, sharing his ham with her when she asked for it. By the time they were finished eating off their plates, the man had left, and he'd had a refill of his tea and she another glass of milk. She looked at him when his empty plates were taken away.

"Thank you." He said it was his pleasure, but she owed him an explanation. "He thinks I'm a boy and wants me to travel with him."

It took his mind a few seconds to catch up to what she was telling him. When his face heated up, hers did as well. As soon as he was brought his check, minus the pancakes that she'd eaten, the girl had moved out of his booth and was on her way out of the place. He barely caught up with her when she was headed for the outdoor restroom for ladies. She asked him what he wanted.

"Should you be out here alone? I mean, the next guy that comes in to have a nice quiet meal might not be so nice. What would you have done had I not kept your secret? He might have gotten you, too, while you were out here?" She said that she had it handled. "I want to help you. Tell me what I can do, and I'll do whatever it takes to get you off the streets."

"I'm not really in trouble other than I don't have a home to go to. I've been hanging out around here for the past month and have been on my toes since to keep myself safe. I don't know what you could do to help me other than do what you just did and keep me from getting caught by perverts." He asked her how old she was. "Sixteen. Listen, you did me a good deed, and I'm sure that once you get to the pearly gates, you'll have enough bonus points that you can get in without any trouble."

"Where are your parents?" She told him that her mother was in the hospital and her dad was in prison. "Nice family you've got there. Well, I can't leave you alone out here. Why don't I pay for you a hotel room that you can stay in until your mother gets out of the hospital?"

"Sure, and you'll just stay in the room to make sure that I'm all right, too. No thanks." He said that he was serious and wouldn't bother her. "That's what the man said who thought I was a boy that he could fondle. No thanks. I'm not going to a hotel with you, mister. Like I said, you did me something good, and

I'm grateful. But I'm not going to be staying with you indefinitely."

There really wasn't anything he could do for her that wouldn't involve the police, and he didn't want her to run off, never to return, just because he had a burr up his ass. But he really didn't want to leave her there all on her own. He decided to talk to Margaret. She might know something that he didn't, which was saying a lot since he didn't know shit about what was going on.

~*~

Kendrick went home and laid down on the couch. There wasn't anyone home, so he thought he'd enjoy a nice nap before dinner. It had been a long day today, and he was exhausted. Of course, he wasn't getting any sleep either, and that was his fault entirely. He was having bad dreams about Dick getting out of jail and coming after Sharon. He just couldn't shake the feeling that she was going to be hurt, and he didn't know how to make sure it didn't happen.

"There you are." He sat up, just dozing off when he heard the front door open. "I was trying to call you, but I kept getting your service. She said she'd put me through, but I thought you might be busy and didn't want to be bothered."

"For you, I want to be bothered. It's just been a long day, and I needed just a little bit of a snooze before dinner. What are we having anyway?" She told him that they were having dinner with Cass and Conri tonight, and that she had some news about her father. "Good. The longer he stays in jail, the better. I'm hoping forever, but I'll take what I can get."

"How about sex?" He just stared at her, not really sure what she meant. "I want to have sex with you. Cass told me I'd be stronger for it, but that's not the reason why. I'm so in desperate need of you that I find myself waking up in the middle of the night, reaching for you. You're not there for me."

"I told you that it would be up to you when we had sex." She said she'd thought that he was joking. "Two things I never joke about are money and sex. And I want to make love to you all over the house. Sometimes twice."

"That would be nice." She came over and sat on his lap, facing him. "I've thought about riding you all afternoon. Do you have any idea how hard it is to concentrate when all I can think about is having your cock inside of me? It's difficult, let me tell you."

"You should have said something sooner. I would have gladly let you ride me. You can do whatever you wish to my body, and I'd let you." She giggled, and he smiled. "My body is yours to do with what you wish. I've been waiting for this day for ages, it seems. Tell me what you want."

Instead of telling him anything, she leaned forward and kissed him. Wrapping his arms around her waist, he brought her closer to him and deepened the kiss. When she touched her fingers to his neck, it was all he could do not to toss her to the couch and take her. He'd really been wanting her for some time now, and he hoped that she was serious when she said that she wanted him.

Loosening his tie, she unbuttoned his dress shirt and pulled it from his pants. He could feel his cock swelling with need, and when she touched him through his pants, he hissed at her. It was too much and not nearly enough. He wanted her. As he did the same to her blouse, he was shocked to find that she didn't have on a bra. Glad that he had one less thing to worry about, he opened her blouse up and took her breast into his mouth and suckled hard. Her hand tangled in his hair as she held him closer to her body. It was everything that he could have hoped for in making love to his mate.

Helping her pull his pants down to his thighs, she stood up and pulled her skirt off. He had to swallow twice before he thought about breathing again. She was glorious in her nudity. Sharon looked like every dream he'd had of her and more so.

"I want you naked." She was so breathless that he could barely understand her. When she began pulling at his slacks, he helped her get them off him with his briefs. His cock was embarrassingly hard, but right now, all he could think about was being deep inside of Sharon until neither of them could move again. "I want to ride you. Let me have my way with you so that I can come when I need it. You'll take over."

"All right." When she settled over him, he helped her as she slid down onto his cock. Neither of them moved while her body adjusted to his, and he had to hold onto her, or he was going to do just what she didn't want him to do, and that was to take over. When she rolled her hips, putting her breasts right at his mouth, he held her tightly to him as he suckled just at her nipples.

She rode him for what seemed like hours. He tried his best not to take over, but it was hard. His cock needed to empty inside of her, and she wasn't making it easy on him, being as beautiful as she was while making love to him.

When she came twice, he wanted to take her to the floor and take her. But she wasn't finished with him and told him so. As he let her have her way with him, all he could do was hold onto her any place that he could touch her. She was making him crazy with need, and he had a feeling that before it was all over, he was going to be on the brink of insanity and would love the trip as much as he did her. And that was saying a lot.

"Take me." He didn't need to be told twice to make love to her and rolling her to her back on the couch, he touched her everywhere he could reach. Her skin was warm to the touch and soft as silk. Her breasts were small, but her nipples were large and dark. As he pulled her hands up above her head, he made love to her slowly, taking his time so that he could make them both enjoy what she started.

When she came again, he nearly joined her. He wanted this to last, and coming when she did wouldn't satisfy either of them as much as he wanted. As she wrapped her legs around his hips, it was all he could do not to beg her to come again so that he could join her, but he made love to her mouth as much as he did her body. They were one, and he couldn't wait to claim her as his mate by biting her on the shoulder.

Making his way down her throat to her neck, he was surprised by how fast her pulse was beating. The need to mark her was overwhelming, so much so that he had to pull away and take several deep breaths so that he wouldn't pass out. She was too much for him, and he couldn't wait to tell the world that he loved his mate.

The need to mark her was something that he couldn't get out of his mind. Licking a path from her throat to her pulse, he bit down on her hard. While he could hear her cries of pain, he didn't stop until he tasted her blood. When she bit down on his own throat, tearing at his skin until she wounded him. As soon as she sucked on the wound, he came apart in several thousand pieces and slammed back together again three times before his body just shut down.

When he woke, Sharon was sleeping. He could see the bruises on her flesh, and he felt bad for it. But almost as soon as he saw the tiny places where he'd hurt her, they healed up and became pink flesh. Reaching for the blanket on the back of the couch, he tried his best to cover the two of them up. Finally giving up, he was glad that he had at least gotten them semi-covered in the event that someone came into the room. Closing his eyes again, he thought that he could lay like this forever and never wake again. His body was so relaxed that he was sure that he'd be sore when he woke up for good.

The next time he woke up, he realized they were on the floor. They both must have been sleeping well if they didn't notice that they'd ended up on the floor. They were both covered up now, and he was glad for that. The room had a bit of a chill in it now that the nights were getting cooler, and he loved the warm body next to him.

"I have to use the bathroom." He groaned when she asked him to move off her. "I'm serious. I really have to go. You either move or we're going to have a mess right here in the living room."

He moved but wasn't happy about it. His body protested even the slightest of moves, and he was happy that she was gone so that he could moan in his privacy. However, the floor was hard and he wanted his bed. Getting up, pulling his pants over his hips, he started locking up the house so that they could go to bed. He knew that he was going to sleep well tonight.

"We were to go to your brother's tonight. I forgot." He said that he'd understand. "I'm sure he knows, too, that we made love. Do you suppose he'll make fun of us?"

"No. He'll be happy for the two of us." He limped his way to the stairs and held onto Sharon's hand as they went up the stairs. "I'm going to sleep for a month. If I didn't have to work tomorrow, I'd not even set an alarm."

"It's only seven-thirty. I'm sure that we'll both get enough sleep going to bed now." He thought it was much later than that, and she agreed with him. "The way I feel right now, I could agree with you in sleeping until the sun was going back down. Every part of my body is relaxed." He thought that was an understatement. He felt like the weight of the world had been lifted from his shoulders and didn't know why. He was glad that she was going to be stronger and told her that. "I'm glad too. Not that I cared when we were making love. But I do feel much better."

They were in the master bedroom when he realized that he didn't know if she wanted him to sleep with her. She took the question out of his hands when she opened the covers on the bed for him and invited him in. As soon as he was in bed with her, his mind began to work on things that should have been left to the daylight hours.

Holding onto Sharon, he held her to his body as he thought of the things that would happen with Dick. He wasn't going to give up; he knew that, and it saddened him a little that he was going to have to deal with him. Not that he wouldn't if he had to, but he didn't want to make Sharon upset with him for doing what needed to be done a long time ago. The man had to die.

As soon as he knew that Sharon was asleep, he got up. He could have spoken to his brother through their link, but he wanted to talk to him. As soon as he answered the phone, Kendrick apologized for not making it to dinner. After telling him that he understood, nothing more was said about it.

After putting it on speaker phone, he got to listen to what Cass had figured out about Dick and his girlfriend. She hadn't spoken to anyone about it yet, but her gut was telling her that she was on the right track. However, it was going to be up to Conri to figure out if they could get a member of another pack there to see if they could find out something.

"I know that's what is going on, but proving that he was involved with it might take some doing. I think that he's benefiting from the money that she's making, but proving that he knew what the money was coming from might be a bit more difficult to prove." She told him what she'd been able to figure out on her own and was now looking for help. "It might not get him prison time, but it will be enough for him to have to go back to New York and face the music. I'm all for getting him out of Ohio if I can get him out. He's going to be nothing but trouble, and I'm sick of having to deal with him."

"I am as well. I think that Sharon is terrified of him, but she doesn't say anything. She's not been sleeping well either." Conri said he could understand that. "I knew that you would. Now all we have to do is prove that he's up to no good and have him extradited back to his home state, and that will be more difficult for him to get back here. I'm assuming you have a plan."

"I don't. I wish that I did, but not yet. I think I have to have proof that he and his girlfriend are in on this kind of work for now, but after that, I'm going to need some help. I'm hoping that he confesses. Wouldn't that be great?" They all three laughed. "I'll have more when Conri gets the other pack leader to help him out. For now, all we can do is hope that this is enough to keep him in jail until I get some evidence. After that, we'll have to play it by ear."

After talking to the two of them more, he was in a better frame of mind. At midnight, he made his way back up to bed and found that Sharon hadn't moved. Smiling, he got into bed with her and was glad that she wrapped her warm body around his. This is the way that he wanted things to go and was glad that she was his for all their lives together.

Chapter 8

Richard was going to have his day in court in the morning. He'd heard that the judge was a good one in that he didn't sentence people too harshly. He didn't want any charges at all from him, so he thought it would be a simple case of in and out. That's what he'd thought all along, and he was still in the system two weeks later.

Looking around his cell, he figured it could have been worse. At least right now, he had a blanket for nighttime and food when he wanted it. In addition to three meals a day, they'd bring around snacks for the inmates so they didn't have to starve between meals. That was his favorite part of his stay here. All the snacks he could eat.

Any day of the week, he'd eat snacks over a meal. A meal would weigh him down, while a bag of chips would be perfect for him to munch on. He even preferred dessert over having supper some nights. A nice slice of cake would fill him like nothing else would. Even if he'd just stuffed himself with a huge meal and could barely breathe around it, he'd make room for some pie every time.

"Richard Taylor, you have a guest." Guest? They'd been calling them visitors since he'd been here. He had no idea what to expect when he was told that he had a guest. Going with the man, he was taken to a cell without cuffs on and sat in a chair. He didn't make a move because the officer in the room with him had his hand on his gun like he meant business. No way was he fucking with a cop. That was when he noticed that the uniform had a state outline of New York and not Ohio. His balls tucked themselves right inside his ass hole.

"We've been talking to Helena Croft." He didn't even blink. Talking to her meant that she'd given him up. "Boy, she has some stories to tell. We've arrested her and the ten people who worked for the two of you."

"I want a lawyer." The cops in the room stopped talking, but he knew they were far from finished with him. "I want a lawyer before I will say another word."

Both of the cops moved out of the room, but for the one who had his gun on his hand. He stared at him like he was just waiting for him to blink so he could blow his head off. Taking his time stretching, he made sure not to make any sudden moves that would get him dead. Even when he had to scratch his head, he did it slowly and precisely where it itched. He wasn't stupid, nor was this the first time he'd been left with a man who seemed to be on a mission to bag him a bad guy.

If they had talked to Helena, then they knew about the prostitution ring that they'd been running. Not even telling them that he didn't know anything about it would get him anywhere, so he was just going to stop talking and wait for a lawyer. They'd had a good run at it, but did wonder how they'd been caught. It had been perfect as far as he could see.

The two of them would set up dates for their herd and give them to them once a day. All they had to do was follow one rule and not all show up at one time, where it looked like they were running a ring. Helena would set up the appointments and make sure that they knew where to go, and he'd collect the money and be the heavy when it was necessary. After the second time he'd had to hospitalize one of their group, he'd never had so much as a peep out of them. And they didn't skim the money either. That was his job, too. Collections.

They'd been doing it for about five years now, and it never ceased to amaze him how much people would pay for a little pussy. Or cock. They weren't judgmental when it came to dates. So long as you had the money to pay and didn't knock around your date too much, things were all right between them.

But they never seemed to have any money. He knew that the rental from the apartment came out of the date money. Also, food as well as utilities. One day, they'd have about twenty-five grand, and the next, they'd be broke. Pulling in six figures a month would have been a good pay off, but they couldn't seem to save any money. Not once in a week could he count on money being there when they needed it. They just liked to spend money.

Helena liked to order things online. She had a closet full of clothing and shoes that she never wore but owned. He wasn't as bad. He didn't have a great many clothes, but he collected weapons. That meant too if they got into the apartment to talk to Helena, then they would have found his stash of guns and knives. All things he wasn't supposed to have being out of prison like he was. Being an ex-con had more rules than he knew how to manage.

He was taken back to his cell, but inside of just putting him inside of it and going away, his gun holder—robocop, he was going to call him—was standing outside his cell and watching him. If he had to take a piss right now, he'd have to do it with a full audience. This shit was for the birds, and he was going to complain about his lack of privacy.

Richard kept going back to how they figured it out. They'd been so careful. He supposed it might have just been the right place, right time sort of thing, but he didn't believe in that. Someone had tipped them off, and he wanted to know who. He thought about asking robocop about it, but he'd not tell him squat. He'd just have to wait until his day in court again before he would be able to figure out any details about when they were caught and who it was that told on them. It couldn't have been the neighbors. They were getting free rent out of the deal, and it was too good of a deal for them to have ratted them out. The landlord was in on it as well, so it wouldn't be him. When he figured it out, hell was going to be paid as they'd taken every precaution they could think of not to get caught.

"It was me and my family that got you caught." He looked around his cell, trying to find the person who was talking to him. *"You can't find me. I'm not there. I've been in your mind for the last week, and let me tell you, it's not been fun. However, we did get the information that we needed about what you're doing for money. So thank you for that."*

"I'm not talking to you. I've asked for a lawyer." The man laughed, but robocop didn't think it was so funny and told him to shut up. "What are you saying to me? You started talking to me."

"It's not robocop, either. If you keep talking to him out loud, he's going to shoot you. I think he wants to anyway." Richard looked around again and couldn't see anyone around. *"I'm not there, I told you, but at my home enjoying a good breakfast with my wife. Your daughter. You should*

know, too, that she's excited to have you going back to New York for your trial. I know I'll sleep better at night."

"How are you doing this?" He was told to shut up again. "How are you talking to me without being around. I demand answers."

Robocop looked about as pissed off as he was feeling. When the man told him once again where he was, he wanted to have him there with him so that he could slap the piss out of him. Instead, he was told how to talk to the man so that no one would know what he was doing. He tried it then. This was one of the more stupid things he'd ever done in his life, talking to a man who was in his head.

"What do you mean you told on me? How is that even possible?" He told him that he knew about it, so it was easy for him to get the information from his mind. *"So you've read my mind? That's not possible."*

"It is, and I'm telling you that it was easy to get into your little cubby holes of lies, too. Do you ever tell the truth?" He said he was going to kill him. *"Another lie. You can't kill me, I'm immortal. So is Sharon. Your plans to kill us both off to get the money would never have worked."*

"So says you. I know better. No one is immortal." The person didn't say anything, and he felt like he'd won that argument. *"I'll be back from New York. You just wait and see. They'll not be able to hold me because they don't have enough evidence. I know the law better than they do. They need evidence in order to take me back, too."*

"*They have all they need. They've been watching your place for a month now, and we just happened to have more information than they did. Like, for example, they didn't know that the entire complex was making out on the little jobs that you were doing. That's why you're so broke all the time. You were paying out more than you were making. You should have hired an accountant when you started out, and they might have told you that it wasn't worth the prison time for as little money as you had in profits. My brother told me that you were shorting yourself every week, paying everyone else's rent and not your own.*" He told him that was the deal they made with them so that they'd not rat them out. "*Yet they did when you refused to pay more money to them. Sorry that it didn't work out for you. But you're going to prison for a lot longer than you had before.*"

"*Why did you do all this?*" He told him why. "*Just so I'd not try and take your money? That was mine, and you owe it to me for all the shit that's going down now. I want a million dollars before my trial so that I can pay my way out of jail. Then you can give me a million every time I want some cash until you die.*"

"*Not going to happen, I'm afraid. I told you before that I'm not giving you any of our money. I like being a wealthy man, and sharing with someone like you doesn't make me feel good about myself.*" He asked why he should care how he feels. "*Because I'm the one who has all the money that you want. You should have just asked for it. I wouldn't have given you any, but I would have gone about getting you out of my hair a lot easier on you."* He asked him if he meant prison. *"Oh no, you'd have gone to prison or died, either one would have been good with me, but I might not have put you away for so long. You're going to be gone for a long time, thanks wholly to all the guns you had in your apartment. That was just stupid of you. From what I've gathered, you get years added onto your sentence for every gun and weapon you have. That's going to be about a thousand years, I'm thinking."*

Robocop told him it was time to go talk to his lawyer. He didn't know what he'd say to the man, he was going to prison for a long time, and he didn't even have any deals he'd like to cut with them. As soon as he was seated across from a man he'd never met before, he broke down. This wasn't the way things were supposed to go for him. Richard was supposed to have everything that he wanted and all the money in the world. Now he was going back to prison, and they might not let him out until he was too old to care about money.

He was told to plead guilty to all charges and hope that he didn't get life without parole. Since this was his third time going to prison, they could throw the book at him, and there was very little that he could do about it. His life sucked right now, and he blamed it squarely on his daughter's head.

"She did this to me." The lawyer, he didn't even ask his name, asked him who he was talking about. "My daughter. She has all the money and won't even share it with her own father."

"You didn't ask, you demanded, correct?" He asked him how he knew that. "I've seen your kind before. You want what she has, and you don't care how you were going to get it. Is that about right?"

"She should have wanted to share with me." The man just nodded like he'd heard it all before. "What do you know? She's worth millions of dollars, and I only wanted my fair share of it. She didn't have to give it all to me." Which was another lie he told himself. He wanted it all and for her to keep paying until she was as broke as he was most of the time.

He didn't even know how he was supposed to have taken it from her. It wasn't like he could have forced her to turn it over. He didn't have any special power to make her do it. He just wanted it and expected her to turn it right over to him without a word. Like that was going to happen, he told himself.

"Someone should have pointed that out to me before. How was I supposed to make her turn over the money when she had lawyers and shit doing what she wanted." He asked if he'd spoken to a lawyer. "Just you. And I'm sure you would have told me to leave her alone, wouldn't you have? Like that would have stopped me. I told her that I was going to kill her when I couldn't even get close enough to her to see what color eyes she had. I should have been told."

"Like you said, it wouldn't have done you any good. You were hell bent for leather on trying to get her money, and no one would have been able to convince you otherwise. You had to learn that lesson on your own." He told him he was still going to try to get something from her. "I doubt that it would work. People get rich because they're smart enough to keep it. You wouldn't have been able to get past them to get a quarter. And you trying would have gotten you killed. No, you're better off not getting the money. You might well live longer in jail had you just given up. Who was that, anyway, that you tried to rob?"

"The Valley men." The lawyer whistled and shook his head. "I guess you might have heard about them being from around here."

"You bet we've all heard about them. And they're not worth millions but billions upon billions of dollars. They own more stock and gems in one state than most people do all over the world. You were right in not getting money from them. People have been trying for decades to get a piece of them. To no avail." He said that his daughter was married to one of them. "If you've gotten on their bad side, then I'd say even that wouldn't get you into their realm of family money. They hold family dear to them unless you screw up. And I'm assuming that you have. Screwed up, I mean."

"I guess I did." He was more depressed than he'd ever been, and now he knew that his plans of being king of the mountain weren't going to happen either. "I don't suppose you'd ask them for bail money for me, would you?"

"I can ask, but I'd not count on it." No, he wouldn't either. Richard was going back to prison, and there was little to nothing he could do about it. "I tell you what, I'll ask and see what happens. What do you say?"

"I'd say he's going to laugh in my face." He reached out to the man he'd been talking to earlier and asked for bail money. The laughter was all the answer he needed to tell the young man with him to forget it. He was getting no help from that quarter.

~*~

Kendrick felt good about himself. He'd done what he'd set out to do and got Dick out of their lives. The very fact that it had cost him nothing was an unexpected bonus that he'd not counted on. He looked at Sharon when she said his name.

"Are you still talking to him?" He told her he'd asked for bail money. "I hope you turned him down. Like I want him out and about terrorizing us until he gets back to his place. I'm to understand that he's going back today."

"Yes. I don't know all the charges, but the gun stipulation is going to get him the most time. I didn't know that once you were an ex-con, you were forever one. I mean, about the guns that he had. He had a lot of them, too. They were stashed all over the house and garage." Sharon asked about Helena. "I don't know much about her at all. I tried to pay attention to the charges, but she has a lot going against her, too. I don't know the law as well as Conri does, and he said that he doesn't have the charges all down pat anyway. I'm just hoping for life. With that, he'll serve at least twenty years, I'm hoping. I did hear one of the officers say that this is his third time in prison, so I'm not entirely sure what's going to happen with that. I was only an attorney for a short time, and I didn't care for it. That's why I became a doctor."

For the rest of the morning, he monitored Dick. He was told to plead guilty to all charges in order to get a reduced sentence, but he didn't know by how much. The cop who was in charge wanted him to go for several life sentences, but he didn't know how that was going to work. He'd only been running a successful prostitution ring and not killed anyone. That he knew of anyway. The man in charge had been watching the place for a month before he'd called in a tip and was happy that things were going as well for him as they could. The entire complex was going to be arrested before things were over. It was all over the local newspaper and his hometown paper on how he'd been caught with the goods.

Kendrick was at work when he heard from Dick again. He wanted to know if Sharon would fill his bank for him at the prison. He didn't know what she'd want to do and told him that. Dick said that otherwise, he was going to have to get a job. Kendrick told him that he should apply for the job; he wasn't going to be lazy while he was in the prison.

It sounded like he was ready to go to prison if he was making arrangements for his bank for snacks and such. It was going to be hard on him this time, as he was much older and didn't get around as well as he used to. Kendrick had noticed, too, that his knees seemed to be hurting him, but never said anything. The few times he'd seen him around town, he'd also noticed how gray the man was. Even his beard, a short, taken care of one, was white gray colored.

"You won. The least you can do is provide me with a few snacks to have when I'm back in prison." Kendrick told him he was never in a position to lose. *"I thought you'd say that. I don't know how I was going to make this work with you two. I had high hopes that you'd just turn the money over to me and be done with me."*

"I'm smarter than that. I've been around a good long time and don't mess with people who think that I'm a sap and will give my money away. I never had any intentions of giving you anything. I would have ended up killing you for sure, so you should count yourself lucky that it didn't come to that. I would have made you suffer." He pointed out that he was suffering now. *"Not nearly as badly as I would have played with you as my wolf. I would have killed you after I got bored with you, but not before. You're lucky that you ended up where you are and not dying by my hand."*

After a few more minutes of silence, he worked with his patients. It was a good day so far, and he thought a great deal of it had to do with Dick going away. He didn't really care if he went to prison or not, just so long as he stayed away from his family and home. But especially Sharon. She was napping when he called her at noon.

"I feel as if a great burden has been lifted from my shoulders." He told her he was glad that she was feeling better. "I am too. I don't have to worry about him anymore, and it feels good. I'm glad that we were able to help the police with their case, too."

"I am as well. There is no telling how long they would have been on the case had we not given them the information that we had. And the very fact that the entire complex is in on it sounds like the case is going to be much bigger than anyone thought." She said she was glad that people were paying for their crimes. "Yes, me too."

For the rest of the day, he talked to Sharon off and on through their link. Once, when she contacted him, he was in the middle of taking blood from a patient and had to have her wait. He didn't want to lose his concentration while doing that, so she contacted him later. He loved that he could talk to her anytime he wanted, and she seemed to be happy with the arrangements as well.

At the end of the day, he was glad it was Friday. Since he wasn't on call this weekend, they were going to hang out at the house and do some things that they'd been putting off. First and foremost was putting the books on the shelves in his office. The boxes were in the way, and he thought that once they got that finished up, he'd feel better about using his office. Just as she'd said she'd do, Sharon set up her office in the library, and it was working out well for her. She was having a good time working with his mom, too. The three of them, Cass included, seemed to be best of friends with each other, and he couldn't have been happier for them. He was just finishing up for the day when he had a call from the hospital. They wanted him to come in and cover a shift for the doctor who had just lost his mother.

"I'll be right in." He couldn't turn him down

when he would have done the same thing for his own mom. Having her around all these years had made him realize how much she'd been a part of his life. "Is there anything going on right now that I have to see to?"

"Nothing so far. We just wanted to make sure you could do this shift for him and not have any trouble. Thank you for helping us out." He said it was his pleasure to help a fellow doctor and headed into the hospital after talking to Sharon. "There are only three people in the emergency room right now, but it's still early. I don't expect much, but you never know with people."

"Yes, I can understand that." He was at the emergency department in no time and was glad that he didn't have a lot to do. It had been a good day at the office, and he was happy that he'd been able to not have to work too hard as he was going to be at the hospital for the next several hours.

As he was seeing one of the patients, he thought about how much he loved being a doctor. But he was ready to try something else. He wasn't bored with his job, just jaded, he thought. Maybe he needed to become something else in the medical field. He'd always wanted to be a surgeon and thought that might be the next thing that he tried. He'd had enough experience as being a doctor; he thought that this was the next step in his journey to being something that he'd never tried before. He was giving it a good amount of thought as he saw his next patient.

He was exhausted when he got home that night. Or the early morning, he wasn't sure what to call it. As he was getting ready for bed, Sharon got up and told him that she'd leave him to his sleep. He wanted her to rest with him, but he knew that it would be selfish of him to ask her to do that. Almost as soon as he laid down, his body decided that it was daytime and he should be up and moving. Tossing and turning for a while, he finally got up and took a shower. He was ready to face the day when he heard from Yuri.

"I have all the paperwork finished up for your investments. You've done really well this quarter." He thanked him for that. "You've had some good ideas on investments, and I'm glad that you had me go in with you. I've had a good quarter as well." They both laughed.

He told him about how he'd been at the hospital all night and was just now getting up and getting going. Yuri said he'd not keep him, only wanted to tell him that his spreadsheet was ready for him to look over, and that was all.

"Thanks for doing this for me. I'm glad that you've been good at your job." He told him how he was going to become a surgeon or something along those lines because of him being jaded. "I've got a lot of experience under my belt, so I don't think I'll have too much trouble going from country doctor to surgeon. I've been wanting to try something different for a while now, and I think this will be perfect. I'll have to go back to school, but I don't think I'll mind that all that much. I love learning new things."

"Then you should go for it. I'm loving my job and doubt that I'll ever get bored with it. I love it when a column of numbers adds up the way they're supposed to and celebrate when they do. I don't go out or anything like that, but I do have myself a little dance around my office." He laughed. "If you tell anyone that, I'll deny it with my last breath. I don't dance all that well, and I would be hard-pressed not to fight you if you were to say anything."

"I promise I won't say a word, but I would like to see you dancing around. I bet it's a sight to be held." The two of them laughed, and he felt better for it. "I'm going to be running on empty soon. I'm glad that you called.

After going to get himself something to eat, he was ready to tackle the books in his office. There were a lot of them, and he knew that he'd get them started before resting a while. There seemed to be an endless supply of books about his line of work, and he was going to love going back to school and learning something new. As soon as he emptied the first of several boxes that were on the floor, he felt better about getting the job done. He only hoped that he'd last until he got all the boxes emptied before he needed a nap.

Chapter 9

Yanick didn't have any luck finding out who Margaret was. He supposed he might have put them off when he demanded information, but he was worried for the kid and wondered if there was anything more he could have done for her. He did leave money for her at the restaurant and his business card with his home number, as well as his personal cell phone number on the back. Now here he was back at work again, and no closer to finding out anything than he had before.

"I'm going to need you to cover for me in the morning. I have something I have to do, and you're the only one who isn't working." He told his boss that he already had plans, knowing that if he came in for the man, he'd have to work two doubles in a row before he came back to work. It was just like him to wait until the last minute before saying anything about it. "I don't care what you have plans. My plans are more important simply because you work for me."

"Well then, how about if I don't?" He asked him what he meant. "I mean, what if I decided that I've had enough working for you and want to branch out on my own. Or do nothing for a while. Whatever I want."

"You're joking." He said nothing but stared at the man. "All right, you can have tomorrow night off. I'll find someone to cover for you if I can."

"No. I told you that I had plans, and I'm not breaking them at this late date." He didn't have anything planned other than to have lunch with his brothers tomorrow afternoon, but he wasn't going to do it. This might just be the push that he needed to get out of this dead-end job. "You'll have to either work yourself or find someone else to do your shift. I don't care."

"Now see here. I'm your boss, and if you don't show up in the morning, I might just fire you." He took off his apron and said that he was finished. "What do you mean you're finished? You get back here before I have to do something drastic. And I'm not kidding you when I tell you you're not going to like it."

"Do what you wish. I'm finished working for you and this place." He was nearly to the door when he was jerked back by his shoulder. "Remove your hand, or I will. And trust me when I say you're going to regret it if I have to remove it."

He removed his hand, and Yanick headed toward the door again. Just as he was getting out into the sunshine, hating that things had come to this but glad for it as well, he got in his car and headed home. The closer he got to his house, the better he felt about things. He was unemployed but feeling like the world was in alignment for him.

Stopping at the restaurant where he'd found the kid, he had himself a big meal and downed it with several glasses of iced tea. He didn't even mind that it was sweet tea; everything tasted so much better now that he wasn't working. Getting someone to tell him about the kid didn't even bother him because he knew that he'd done everything he could to help her out. He left more money for her in the way of the cook and was on his way again.

Getting to his house, he changed out of his work things and put on a pair of jeans and an old t-shirt. He was ready to get some work done and was ignoring his phone. It had rang several times since leaving work, and he figured that if anyone important wanted to get in touch with him, then they'd reach out.

He had just finished cleaning out his pantry when he decided to check his phone. There were fifty-one messages and several phone messages. He listened to them all because it gave him something to laugh about. The voice mails were getting angrier and angrier as time went on. It wasn't until he got to the last of them that he realized that he really did feel good about quitting. It wasn't his fault, not that he would not take the blame later for it happening the way that it had, but he really did feel better about what he'd done.

Making himself something to eat, he was happy that he'd gone to the store the day before. He'd thought about ordering something in, but he wanted to cook for himself. After dinner, he cleaned up his mess and went to the living room. There he sat and watched a movie that he'd not seen in ages and took a nap. He was just getting up when Conri reached out to him.

"*I just heard from your boss. He said that there had been a misunderstanding and that you'd left work early. He wants you to call him. I take it that you finally quit.*" He said that he had, and he felt good about it. "*Good for you. I'm glad for you. I hope that you take some time off before you get back into things. You're not going to go back to that toxic place, are you? I think if you bitched about your job much more, I was going to quit for you.*"

"I'm not going back. I've burnt that bridge. And even if I didn't, I'm done with it. He really was toxic." He told him what had happened to make him quit today. "I would have had to cover for him for several days, as his time planned never included just one shift. I've done that before and didn't care for it."

"*What do you want me to tell him when he calls again? I'm assuming that he's reaching out to your brothers, too. I can well imagine what they might say to him. We've been worried about you for some time now.*" Yanick said he was sorry. "*I'm not. I'm glad for you. So is Cass. She said that you'll feel better about life again now that you don't have to go there to work. And that you might find your mate with you not working so hard. I had no idea that you were working that hard until she pointed out that you were forever canceling dinner engagements in order to cover a shift or two. Like I said, I'm happy that you've done this."*

"I'll probably feel guilty tomorrow for leaving them short-staffed, but I find that I don't care today. So long as I can find me another job in about a month, and I see no problem with that, then I'll be all right. I just got my quarterly reports back from Yuri, and I'm doing much better than I thought that I was." He said that he'd had a good quarter as well. "We should celebrate sometime soon. My treat. I'm unemployed, so perhaps we can make it cheap."

They both laughed, and it felt good to be laughing about something that should have been really serious. He'd pick up the tab no matter where they went and be happy about it. His family was all that he had, and he was happy that they all got along so well.

He knew that he'd have to call his mom later and let her know. For all he knew, she might have been as upset with him about the job as the others were. He'd not realized that they were rooting for him to quit, or he might have done something sooner. But he did like the way things had worked out. He didn't even care that he was going to be painted as a bad employee from all this. It was done and over with, and he was glad for it.

Getting his cabinets cleaned out was next on his list of things that he'd been wanting to get done. Tossing out things that were expired, he realized that he rarely cooked at home anymore. Or anywhere for that matter. Just at his job, and he'd had enough of that. As he was putting things back away, he made a list of things he was going to need to pick up. He might as well get fully stocked up if he was going to be doing things around his house for a change.

By midnight, he was ready to call it quits. He'd gotten done more than he thought he would and felt proud of the fact that he'd been able to get a good list of things that he was going to need too. Not only had he gotten his kitchen organized and ready for groceries, but he'd finished up his laundry and changed the sheets on his bed. Laughing to himself, he thought that he'd make a good mate to someone soon with all the domestic stuff he was getting done.

Going to bed around one, he was exhausted but in a good way. Like he wasn't mentally knocked out, but physically. He'd gotten a lot of work done and was proud of himself, but he'd also gotten his mind off quitting his job. He didn't feel the least bit sad for it either. Just good that he'd finally gotten his life together.

Waking in the middle of the night when his cell

phone went off, he answered it on the second ring. Surely it wouldn't be work calling him, and he was surprised when no one answered his hello. Waiting for just a few seconds, he was ready to hang up when he heard a whispered voice at the other end.

"It's Margo. I'm the kid you shared your pancakes with." He whispered back to her if she needed him. "I do. I'm in trouble here, and I don't think my stellar personality is going to get me out of this one."

"I'm on my way. I'm assuming that you're still at the restaurant." She said that she was, but for him to hurry. "I'm getting my keys now and am on my way. I'll be there in less than an hour."

"I'm out back by the dumpsters. Hopefully, I'll still be there when you get here. I'm hiding from a drunk." He was pulling out of his driveway when she spoke to him again. "I'm moving again. When you get here, I'll come to you. I don't want you to get your fancy clothing all messed up because you had to save me."

"I'll beat your ass if you get caught." She laughed, but it was cut off when he heard a crash. "What's going on? Where are you hiding?"

"I'm hiding. Just get here. You're my only hope of surviving." He didn't like that thought, but couldn't say anything as she'd cut off the connection between the two of them. Pushing a little harder on the gas pedal, he was getting on the highway about ten minutes from his home when he realized that he knew her name now.

Pulling into the lot about thirty minutes after hearing from her, he didn't know what to do. There was a truck running in the lot, so he left his own running. He was just getting out of the car when someone got into his car. Letting out a long breath, he asked Margo if she was all right.

"I've been hurt. Does your generosity extend to taking me to the hospital? I think I'm going to need to see someone about my head. It hurts a great deal." He pulled out of the parking space he'd been in and then stopped. "What are you doing?"

"He's coming toward us. And I, for one, would like to see what a grown man wants with a sixteen-year-old kid." She just looked at him. "All right, I know what he wants, but it doesn't do much for my temper right now. Stay in the car, and I'll have a little talk with him."

As soon as he got out of the car, he could smell the man. He was a wolf, too, and he must have known that he was the brother of the Alpha. It was hard to miss as he would smell like someone powerful, and the idiot had to understand what he was dealing with.

"I'm taking her to the hospital. I have your scent now, and if she's hurt very badly, I'm coming back here to hunt you down." He said that he wanted her. "I don't care what you want. I'm taking care of her now, and you'll back off before I have to kill you."

"She's been teasing me all month. I want what she's been offering me." He said she was just a kid and was not offering him anything. "Be that as it may, I'm taking her and there ain't shit you can do about it. Just dump her out of the car and drive away. This doesn't concern you."

"It does now." Yanick waited to see if he'd do anything stupid, but he should have known better. The man was all kinds of stupid for taking him on, but as soon as he shifted, Yanick did the same thing. It was over almost as soon as he did that. The man lay dead in the parking lot, and he wasn't going to be able to shift back without causing all kinds of trouble for himself. The man had lost his head when he ripped out his throat, and the police were going to want to know what happened.

"You killed him." He stared at Margo when she got out of the car. "I'm not even going to say that I'm sorry that it had to come to that. He's been trying to hurt me for over a month now. I'm guessing that you can't shift back without being naked."

He had no connection with her and went to her. If he could make her understand that he needed to bite her, then he could tell her to call the police. Instead of wanting to make her understand, she put out her hand, and he bit down into the softest part of her hand. It was all that he needed to be able to talk to her. While she called the police, getting his clothing out of his trunk as she did, he reached out to his brother and let him know that he was going to be arrested for killing a man.

~*~

After declaring the man dead, he examined the kid. That's what Yanick had been calling her since they all arrived, and he didn't know if he'd ever heard her name or not. So far, he'd found out that she had a concussion and several broken ribs. No wonder she'd called for help. He wasn't sure she would have survived if the man had gotten her again. With him being a wolf, he was doubly stronger than her and would have gotten what he wanted no matter how hard she tried to get away. Conri wasn't happy about things either.

"I'm not worried about you being in trouble with me. You saved a kid, and I'm proud of you. But the police are going to want answers for a dead man, and I don't know what to tell them." Yanick told them that he'd been questioned quite a bit, but they'd never charged him with anything. "I think they're waiting on the cause of death to be said out loud. No one can disagree that he's had his head removed, but I think they're wondering how it happened. You told them about the kid?" Yanick nodded, then pointed to the kid.

"She did as well. I've been trying to find her for the past week, but she's been hiding well. And the people in the restaurant never said a word about her being targeted. I'm assuming they had to know, as they all seem to know her well enough." The owner of the restaurant had shown up about an hour after they arrived to verify that Margo did work for him. He also said that she'd been having trouble with this man for a while, too. "If they had told me, I would have done something more. But with them not telling me anything, all I could do was wait until she contacted me."

"You're going to be all right, Yanick. If nothing else, they'll just have you say that you found him in the lot looking like he did. I don't think they're going to lose any sleep over him being dead. I guess they'd had complaints about him chasing the employees for about a couple of months now." He'd not known until Conri said something that three of the officers were wolves, too. And one of them was a tiger. "What we have to do is cooperate with them and see how they want to handle this. I'm just glad that the kid is all right."

"I need to get her to the hospital to make sure that her concussion is all right. I mean, it's not, but she also has some broken ribs that worry me a bit." He asked if they were going to allow her to leave. "I don't know. I've asked, but they keep putting me off. I'm thinking that they're waiting for their alpha to come and see to his body."

"That would be my assumption. He'll have to be notified about his death if he hasn't already been. Then from there we'll figure out what's going on." Kendrick knew that someone was going to be declaring the homicide justified, and as soon as the alpha said that it was clean, then the police would work to make it look like it. It wasn't legal, but it would keep Yanick out of jail for now. "I think he's just arrived. Just so you know, I told him that you made contact with the girl a week ago. He knew about the trouble they were having here, but didn't know it was one of his."

"He should have done something about it." They all agreed but didn't voice that so that he could hear. Yanick was upset, probably more than a little pissed off that he'd had to kill the man, but he was waiting his turn to speak when the other alpha shook hands with Conri.

"You don't have to worry about any of this, young Valley." He was older than the man, and he thought that he knew it. "I'll take care of any fines that need to be paid to the police for calling them out so late tonight."

"What about the girl? She's been dealing with this man for over a month now, and nothing has been done about it." David Attobone, the alpha, said that he'd known there was trouble; however, he'd not known that it was one of his wolves. "Would you like to tell me why not?"

"Sure. I have a large pack, and while that's no excuse, I do want you to know that I'm going to make sure that the girl wants for nothing. She's been hurt as badly as I have been about this, and I'll make sure she's taken care of. She won't face any consequences either."

"That's enough for now." Yanick looked at him before looking at David again. "She needs to go to the hospital. As soon as you approve it, she can go in the ambulance. I hope that won't be a problem."

"No. Had I known you were waiting for me to take her in, I would have said something before I arrived. As it stands right now, neither of you will be fined, and it will be an unsolved murder, but for the pack. They'll know that he's been dealt with." Yanick didn't seem satisfied with his answers but backed off for now. He'd killed a man, and he looked like he'd do it again if pushed. "I'll be in touch with you soon, alpha. I'm sorry that it came to this. Especially for your friend."

David didn't leave like he thought he would. But hung around with the police to make sure that things were taken care of. When the report was given to the station police head, it was said that his body had been found like that, and they'd help with finding a way to find his murderer. Nothing would be done about it if the pack didn't make a fuss, and that's the way it should have been done.

~*~

Kendrick accompanied Margo to the hospital. He had finally found out her name and wasn't privy to the rest of what happened at the scene after that. Once he was there with her, it was as if they'd been expecting her to arrive, and she was taken to X-ray right away. She was also given a private room where he stayed with her and was glad that things weren't as bad as he'd thought. She still had a concussion, but there were only a couple of ribs broken, not as many as six like he'd thought, and she was going to spend the night at the hospital, and the billing was to go to the pack to take care of it.

Once Margo was settled into a private room, he made some calls. He needed to get in touch with Sharon to let her know that things were going to be all right, and then he called his service. Telling them that he was off duty until tomorrow made him feel good. He'd been having a time at home and hadn't wanted to leave. Now he was going to have an excuse for not showing up for work in the morning and was all right with it.

"I'm fine. So is Yanick." Sharon was relieved

and told him so. "I am as well. I was worried as soon as I saw the body. He removed his head with one swipe of his paw. That takes a powerful bit of muscle to do that to someone."

"Or anger. You did say that he'd been keeping an eye out for this girl for a while now." He told her that she was doing all right as well. "Good. You just bring her home with you, and we'll take care of her until we hear something different. Yanick told me that her father was in prison — there seems to be a lot of that going around and that her mom was in the hospital. Perhaps you can have a look while you're there to see if we can help her on the road to recovery."

"I'll do that." As soon as he said that, Margo asked him if he'd do the same thing. He told her that he would. "I have to go now. There are people around that want answers, and I have to be on my toes. The way things are going here, I might not make it back before lunchtime tomorrow. Just don't wait up for me. I don't want us both to be exhausted."

"I'll try not to stay up, but I worry with you being gone. It's different when you're in the hospital around here. You're still an hour from home." He said that she'd been taken to the local hospital when he requested it. "I take it it's not all that far from where the other place is then."

"No, it's the same distance from where we were.

The alpha approved her going to the hospital where I work so that I could take care of her." She said she was happy with that. "I'm going to get off here now. I can see Conri and the others now, and it won't be long. I'll see about seeing Margo's mother while I'm here."

He didn't have any trouble seeing her mom, but there was no hope for her in getting out of the hospital soon. She had stage four cancer throughout her body, and her organs were beginning to shut down. He told Margo what was going on, and she seemed to understand. She said that her mother had been sick for a while now, and the doctor told her that there wouldn't be much more they could do for her but to keep her comfortable.

At dawn, he was headed home. Sharon was up, but she'd only just gotten out of bed when he arrived. After kissing her on the mouth, he told her that he only wanted to lie down for a little while, as he didn't want to sleep all day. Almost as soon as the lights were off in their room, he was sleeping. He'd not been this tired from working in a long while.

Waking at noon when his alarm went off, he had a message from Margo. She was released to go home today and wondered if he'd come and pick her up. She would have asked Yanick to take her home, but he was stressed out enough.

"My home isn't really a home so much as a shed

that has a car in it. I've been staying in it for about a year now, and that's why I hang out at the restaurant. The food is better, and sometimes I can stay in the apartment above the place if the owner isn't around. If you could pick me up and take me there, I'd appreciate that."

He was going to bring her to his house, and she could stay there. He'd even make sure that she got back and forth to the hospital when she wanted to see her mom. Kendrick did wonder what his brother would say if he knew where she lived. He'd more than likely bundle her up and take her to his house for sure. But he was in a better situation than his brother was in, in that he had a home with bedrooms, whereas Yanick lived in a house, it was only two bedrooms, and one of them was a makeshift office for him.

Making his way back to the hospital, he told his family what his plan was. To keep the kid safe was a high priority for him, and he wasn't going to take no for an answer. She needed help, and he was in a position to help her as much as she'd allow him to. He really didn't expect her to allow him to do too much for her, but he was going to be there for her if she needed him. All he had to do was convince her that he was her safest bet right now.

The hospital was busy when he arrived. There was no talk about the dead man from last night, and he

Kathi S. Barton

was surprised to see that the alpha was still there. When he spoke to him, he told him that he was taking care of Margo and then told him about her living situation and her mom. He wasn't happy that he couldn't take her into his home as well as Kendrick had it all covered.

Kendrick took Margo down to see her mother before they left. She held her hand while he was in the room, so he stepped out to give her some privacy. Standing at the door, he wanted to make sure that she had as much time as she needed and was willing to guard the door for her so that she could. When she met him in the hallway, he could tell that she'd been crying, but didn't say anything. She was entitled to her own privacy from him as well.

The drive home didn't take very long. The two of them talked all the way, and he was glad to know that she'd graduated from high school the year before. There were little bits of information he was learning about her, and he was glad that he'd been able to help her out with this. As soon as they pulled into his driveway, Sharon met them on the porch and welcomed Margo with open arms. As soon as they were in the house, he decided to sit on the bench outside on the porch and rest. He'd not gotten enough sleep today, but he knew he'd be all right. Being home helped, and he was never so happy to be there as he was in that moment.

Margo was given a room, and as he'd gone with

her to pick up some of her things, he knew she'd not be going back there so long as he was alive. It was just as she said, a shed with a car hanging out of the opening of it. He wondered what she did in the winter months and was happy that he'd found her before something else might have happened to her. He liked the kid and was glad that he'd been able to keep her safe at least for now. Kendrick didn't know what tomorrow would bring, but he was going to be here for her today and all the todays that she'd allow him to be.

Chapter 10

Sharon liked having the kid around. She'd gotten in the habit of calling her kid because the rest of the family had. Her name was Margo Pennington, as they all knew her to be, and she was going to stop calling her kid as soon as she could. It wasn't until Ethel, Kendrick's mother, came over that Margo began to open up to her.

"I was taking some college courses when my mom got sick. She was up and around one day, then the next, she was down with the flu. The doctor told me that she had been weakened by the flu, and the cancer took over her body. He told me that she was lucky to have lived as long as she had, as much as it was in her system. Now all I can do is wait for her to die so that I can go back to living in the shed." She didn't tell her that she wasn't going to be living in the shed anymore. Kendrick had described it to her, and there was no way that she was going to be doing that again. It was Ethel who told her she was going to be just fine staying here. "But I have a place to stay that won't put you out."

"Nonsense. You'll stay here with Kendrick and Sharon, and that's all I want to hear about that. You're just lucky that I didn't find out you were living there all alone. I wouldn't have stopped until I found you. Then you'd be right where you belong. Here, as my granddaughter." She didn't say anything, and Sharon wondered if some morning she'd wake up and Margo would be gone. "I don't want to hear about you running off either. I won't take too kindly to having to get the pack involved in your safety. You'll live here and have a wonderful life. Trust me when I tell you that I'm not going to allow you to go anywhere else from now on."

"You can't just tell me where I'm going to be living, you know. I mean, I'm not an adult yet, but I've been taking care of myself for a while now." Ethel said that she'd done a good job so far, but it was time for the adults to help her out. "I don't know how to do that. When I called your son, it was the first time I'd asked for help since my mom had gotten sick. I wouldn't even begin to know how to repay you for what you've done for me so far."

"You pay it forward. That's something that everyone can do. Just pass a bit of wisdom on to someone else. Pay for someone's dinner or something. Just little things to know that you've helped one person that day. I've taught that to my boys all their lives, and that's why I can say for sure that you'll be all right living here with them. They'll never treat you like anything but their daughter, you can count on that."

Margo didn't seem convinced, but that was all right, too. Once she was there for a while, she'd be just fine with staying with them forever. "Also, you might want to think about getting yourself a job. It will go a long way in your getting up on your feet after your mom passes. It'll keep you busy."

"I don't want her to die, but I know that she's suffering." Ethel said that any fool could see that, and she should be grateful that she was getting the medication that she needed. "Kendrick said that she was getting the best meds there were to keep her comfortable. I was afraid they'd let her suffer because we don't have insurance. But they've been taking care of her really well every time I get to see her." She told her that Kendrick wouldn't allow that to happen to anyone. "No, I can see that. You love him very much, don't you, Sharon?"

"With all that I am." She felt her heart swell with the knowledge that she loved her mate that much and wondered why other people didn't have the same kind of love for their mates as she did Kendrick. "He's the best thing that has ever happened to me, and I'm proud to say that I love him out loud too."

"Now we need to go shopping. You should have some other clothing than what you brought with you." Margo said that she was fine. "No, you're not. You don't even have any kind of deodorant in the house. We'll go and get you some supplies so that you can feel at home with yourself. Also, a few extra items of clothing won't hurt either."

"I just need a few supplies. I can get the rest later." But Ethel was moving them out the door, and she couldn't have been happier. She'd never realized how pushy the older woman was until right then and was glad they were on the same side. She'd hate to think what she'd do to her if she disagreed with her about something. They were in the car when they decided to invite Cass along with them to make a girls' day of it. "This is getting too big. I just need some personal things."

They were headed to her favorite place to eat when Cass joined them. The Flower Shop had a nice luncheon menu, and the place doubled as a florist, too. Almost before she sat down with the others, she knew what she was going to get. A nice juicy hamburger with fries sounded the best, and she wanted a malted milkshake to go with it. Sharon was going to test the theory about not being able to gain weight being with a wolf as a mate.

After lunch, they headed to Walmart to grab some personal items for Margo. It never occurred to her how much she would need living with them, and she was glad that Cass had suggested they hit a few of the pretty little boutiques on their way around town.

All Margo had with her were two shirts, another pair of jeans, and some shoes that looked like she'd been wearing them for a few years. They could do a lot better than that.

They had so many bags by dinner time, she was sure they weren't going to be able to fit in the car. Luckily for them, they'd all ridden in the same truck, and that left them plenty of room in the back to stuff with bags and boxes. Margo not only had a lot more pants and shirts, but she also had some pretty dresses as well as shoes to go with each one. Sharon had even brought her some clothing too, as she didn't have much to wear towards the end of summer and into fall. She loved the warm colors, too, that were there for her to choose from.

Cass had purchased some clothing to wear as she got bigger with the baby. It had been fun going through the baby department of each store they'd hit up. She couldn't wait until she was ready to have Kendrick's child. She was going to watch Cass to see how she'd done things, as she didn't have any idea how to be pregnant with a wolf child. A cub it was called.

Going home, they decided to have a grill out tonight with all the family. Their cook was going to be ready for them all, and all that had to be done was cooking the burgers and steaks. The men were going to join them at their house, and it was going to be a good night. The weather had turned cooler, and there wasn't a cloud in the sky. It was a beautiful night to have a cookout, and she was excited about it.

Dropping Margo off at the hospital, Kendrick was going to bring her home. She wanted to tell her mom about her day, and none of the others could blame her. It was nice to have gotten her out and about, and not worrying about where her next meal was going to come from. She couldn't imagine being Margo's age and being on her own. She didn't like it now and was a full-grown adult. Some days, she wished she were still a child so that she could be better prepared for life.

But she'd done all right, she figured. She was in love with someone who loved her back, and she had a roof over her head as well as food that she could eat at any time. She didn't know how much more prepared for life she could have been, but in dealing with her father. But he was gone now, off to prison, and she was working on a relationship with her mom to see where that went. All in all, she thought her life was perfect the way it was.

It was nice having the family over for dinner. They made every time they were together seem so special. They were loving and loud, and she wouldn't trade having them with her for all the money in the world. They were the best set of brothers a girl could ask for. She got a hug from Ethel when she sat down next to her.

"I was just thinking how much our family is going to expand come the holidays. It's been a long time since we've done much more than get together for Thanksgiving. I mean, I don't even think we had a turkey last year, but steaks out on the grill." Sharon said that sounds divine. "It was. The boys did all the cooking, and I was left to my own devices. They all know how to cook, and I'm proud of them. But someday I'd like to have a table full of people down the sides, with it groaning with food. Do you think you can make that happen for me?"

"I can and will do that for you. I don't know how many more wives will be joining us before the holidays, but they'll each and every one be welcome here. Is Christmas a big holiday for you guys? I mean, do you put up a tree?" She said that she had one put up in her place, but they usually met at one of the boys' homes. "No tree, I take it."

"I know that it's the same day every year, but it sort of sneaks up on you. One day it seems like it's Thanksgiving, and the next time you wake up, Christmas and the New Year are here, and there wasn't any time to put up any kind of decorations. It's sad now that I think about it." She told her that it sounded lonely to her. "Yes, it is a bit of that. Usually, Kendrick works for the hospital so that doctors with families can have it off. Yanick used to work for the restaurant that we'd all turn up at so we could see him, but I don't know what his plans are now. I'm so glad he's quit that job. It was wearing on him. The boss thought that he could take advantage of my boy, and he showed him what was going on."

"Yes, I heard. I would have laughed had I been there. I can see Yanick quitting but being so calm about it. Just taking off his apron and leaving. That's so like him." Ethel said he'd only ever quit one other job that she knew of, and it had been just as bad. "I'm sorry to hear that. It sounds like he needs to open his own place so that he can be his own boss. Can I ask you a personal question?"

"Of course you can. Be prepared for the truth. I can't lie to you either, so I won't. But you'll get the answer you might not want." She said she wasn't worried and asked her about the boys' names. "Oh, that's a funny story. I didn't want to name any of them after their father or his side of the family. So I picked a few numbers in a child's naming book and used the names that corresponded to those numbers. Conri is the only name that I picked out. In Gaelic, it means wolf king. I so loved the way that it rolled off my tongue that I knew I had to name him that."

"It suits him. With him being alpha and all. He's

been pack leader for a while now, hasn't he? I mean, longer than I've been alive." She nodded and smiled. "I don't think I want to know how long he's been alpha. He's really good at the job, and I can't think of anyone who is better suited to the job."

"His father was the alpha. But he and Conri's first wife stole from the pack and had an affair. He'd been claimed by me, but she'd never been. So when pack justice was given to the pack, they were both killed. We don't speak either of their names anymore. They're not worth our memories." She said she'd remember that. "Something else you should remember is that pack justice is fast and deadly. When someone is brought before the pack, they usually have all the information they need in order to make their deaths swift. Unless Conri orders it to be painful for them, they're usually dead by the time the first drop of blood is drawn."

Sharon shivered and looked away. She didn't want to think about how someone might die by pack. While she'd not seen anyone die that way, she thought that she could go her whole life without seeing it, too. She went to find Kendrick, as he was home now from work. Smiling up at him, he kissed her on the mouth.

"I was just talking to your mother. We're going to go all out for the holidays this year and from now on. We'll have the biggest tree because we have the room for one." He asked her why she wanted just one tree. "You're right. We'll have one in every room in the house, including the bathroom. I'm excited for Thanksgiving, too. I've been assigned to fill a table with food and have everyone sitting down on either side of the table. I think I can do that with your help."

"I'm all yours. I have both Christmas and Thanksgiving off this year. I didn't ask for it, but someone put my name in for it off. I think it's because I usually work for someone, but this year I'm going to take it off to be with you and my family." She kissed him on the chin, and he laughed. "I do love you, my dear. Very much so."

"And I love you so very much, too. We should take out billboards so that everyone knows how much we do love one another." They were still joking about their love for each other when they entered the dining room. It was the largest room in the house, she thought. All she needed to do was find a table to hold them all. She had four months. She could do it by then, she thought.

~*~

"I'm not sure that I understand. There is no way that I owe that much in back rent." Raven looked over the paperwork she'd been handed and then at hers that she'd been keeping records on. "I know you said it's only a hundred dollars more, but I'm on a tight budget, and I can't afford to pay out anything extra right now."

"Let me go over the numbers again. I can't believe that I'm allowing you to do this. I should have my head examined." Raven just smiled at the man and knew deep down in his heart there was a little bit of goodness. "You owed twenty-five dollars from January, but you were able to get it the next month."

As he went over his numbers, she did the same with hers. Getting caught up today was going to take a huge burden off her shoulders. Winning the lottery last week had helped her with a lot of things, but no one knew that yet. She was taking one step at a time so that no one was any wiser about her winning such a huge jackpot. He found the hundred dollars on his end, and she was relieved. The man had been good to her, letting her slide on rent sometimes for as much as a week. But she had the money now and was going to be caught up for the rest of her life.

Paying her landlord, he seemed satisfied with the way things were going. All she had left to pay was her electric bill and the gas bill that had been shut off in June. She'd been taking cold showers since that day, and now, as of today, she was going to be able to take hot showers year-round. A lot of things were going to be changing for her.

She'd not gone out and spent any of her newfound money on anything but catching up with her bills. There wasn't any way that she was going to buy herself a new television as the old one still worked. She didn't drive, so there would be no fancy car in the lot either. She was going to pay her bills on time from now on and work her job so that she could live a comfortable life without anyone being any wiser that she'd won forty million dollars.

Every time she thought of the amount, she would have to sit down and put her head between her knees. It wasn't just that she'd won some money; she'd won enough money to make a real difference in her life. However, she wasn't going to do that. It would get her in trouble with her family and friends when they wanted a bit of what she'd gotten.

So far, just she and the banker knew about it. Of course, the lottery people knew, but they were kind of pissy about the fact that she didn't want her name to be associated with the check they'd given her. She didn't care. So long as no one knew her name or address, she thought that she'd live a good deal longer. Making her way home to her apartment, she stopped and picked up another lottery ticket as it was Thursday. She bought one every Thursday like clockwork.

She'd never played the same numbers either. She just bought a random ticket and went home with it. Sometimes she'd buy a scratch-off ticket, too, but not too often. It was money that she didn't have until last week.

When she got home, she hung up the ticket on her fridge and did her laundry. The laundry mat wasn't all that busy today, so she was able to use both the washers and dryers at the same time. Folding her sheets, she thought again about how much money she had and what some people would do for it. For a fact, she knew that her family, her brothers, especially, would kill her for it if they knew.

They both worked when they had to, but it wasn't steady, nor did it pay all that well. Usually, they could get a job delivering pizzas — there were plenty of those around, but as soon as they decided that they needed the food more than the customer, they'd be out of a job. They never took her money or anything, but they would crash at her place when they needed to lay low or hadn't paid their own rent. She'd told them once that she couldn't help them if she was out of a place to live, too. So they'd leave her alone with her money and go about their business on their own. But winning the lottery was bigger than even she could imagine.

Tommy would have demanded that she give it over to him, but he would have given her some of it to tide her over. He might knock her around, too, for not telling him right away, but he'd not hurt her too much. It was Sherman that she was most afraid of.

He'd kill his own mother if he thought that she

was holding out on him. In fact, she was sure that he had killed her. But since she could never prove it or even bring it up, she kept her mouth shut and lived for another day or two. When he was around, she'd let him have whatever he wanted in her home. Usually, it was her bed, but she was all right with sleeping on the couch. Tommy would take the chair from her because he was bigger than her. To be so afraid of her family made her ill sometimes.

The knock at her door had her being cautious about answering. Her brothers would knock, but it was more of a pounding than anything else. Opening the door just enough so she could see who it was, she was surprised to find Tommy there holding onto Sherman. He was bleeding from something wrong with his chest, and she moved so that Tommy could lay him on the couch.

"What's happened? Do you want me to call an ambulance?" They both said no, and she had to worry if Sherman was going to die right here in her place. "What's happened to him?"

They worked on getting his shirt off, and she stood by. Just what she needed, a dead man in her place after getting her rent squared away. Once she was able to see the bullet hole in Sherman's chest, she hissed at the amount of blood he was losing. She asked again what had happened.

"You don't need to know." She started to point out that they were in her place, but didn't. Sherman had that look in his eyes like he was on the verge of murder. She'd seen it before. "Get me some towels so that I can wipe myself off."

"I only have three. I know you don't want to hear this, but my landlord isn't going to be happy if you've brought guns to my place. I told you before that this is a good place for me, and I don't bother anyone." He told her again to get the towels. "You can have one."

She got the towel for Sherman and decided that she was going to have to replace them soon. They were threadbare and not in good shape. She wondered if she could get them into her place without anyone noticing. Then she looked at her brothers. She couldn't believe she was worried about towels when her brother might be dying on her sofa. Something else occurred to her, and that she was a millionaire and didn't need to put up with shitty towels or brothers bleeding all over her only good piece of furniture. She stomped her foot, and that had them both looking at her.

"If the police are going to be coming by, I have a right to know. I told you last week that I worked enough overtime to get my rent caught up, and now you're messing things up with me. Tell me what's happened, or leave. I've enough on my mind without you two here making a mess." Sherman swatted at her, but she was too far away for him to touch her. Just as well, he was getting weaker by the moment. "What's happened?"

"I got shot, dumbass." She didn't get hurt that he was calling her names, but she did tisk at him. "I was trying to set something up so that I'd have some money when this guy pulls out a gun and shoots me. I'm sorry that I'm bleeding on your piece of shit couch. Next time I'm hurt, I'll just lie on the road and let people run over me."

"Why did you think to come here?" He said she was closest. "So the police are going to be involved. Great. Just what I need."

"You're uppity all of a sudden. What's got you being lippy with me?" She just pointed to the mess he'd made on her couch. "It's just a bit of blood. You can clean it up. I'm doing all right in the event you were going to ask."

"I can see that you are. You're talking, aren't you?" She wanted to kick them both out, but went to the kitchen instead. "I'm making myself some dinner. If you want something, you're going to have to order out. I only have enough food for myself."

As she made herself a peanut butter and jelly sandwich, she thought about what was going on in the other room. If she wasn't careful, she was going to get caught with the winnings, and they'd never find her body. She had no doubt that with all the things going on with them, they'd knock her around until she was dead, and that would be the end of her money. She was glad now that she'd put it in a safety deposit box in the bank so that no one would find it here in her place.

Tommy came into the kitchen and slapped her hard. If she had not been sitting down, she would have fallen to the floor and hurt herself badly. Instead of crying like she wanted to do, she just stared at him.

"You keep your mouth shut, and I won't have to kill you, too." She wanted to ask him who he'd killed, but thought that she'd live longer if she didn't. "I'm going out for a while, and when I return, he'd better be alive. I'm not shitting you right now. I have enough shit on my mind without you being a bitch. Shut up and do as you're told. Do you understand?"

"Yes." She didn't bother wiping the blood she could feel on her lips. Even the taste of it was something that she tried to ignore. There were plenty of things that she wanted to say, but she kept her mouth shut. Things would go from bad to worse if she were to tell him what she thought of them being here.

When Tommy left, she stayed in the kitchen. She wasn't hungry anymore, so she pushed her plate away and thought about how she could get out of this mess she was in. The only thing that she could think about was just leaving them to her place. She had enough money now that she could afford to get herself a new identity and hide from them the rest of her life. Not having any idea how that was to work, she sat in the kitchen and cried. All the good things that had happened to her were going her way, then her brothers showed up. They were forever fucking up her life, and she hated them both.

After feeling sorry for herself for a little while longer, she decided to clean up the mess she'd made. It wasn't much, just a plate and a knife, but she liked things tidy and cleaned up. She didn't have much, but what she had was hers, and she was going to take care of it. Going into her living room, she sat in the chair and watched her brother sleep. He was either sleeping it off or unconscious, and she found that she didn't care. Lying back on the chair, she thought more of her plan to get away from them.

She must have dozed off because when she woke up, Tommy was back, and he didn't seem happy. But then he rarely seemed happy about things, and she just laid there listening to them talk.

"He's been picked up by the police. I'm thinking that with his record, they'll just write it off as a robbery gone wrong. He won't be missed, that's for sure." Sherman said that he was glad that he was dead. "I am as well. One less prick we have to deal with on this job coming up. Are you going to be able to go? You seemed to have lost a great deal of blood."

"I'll be fine. Just make sure that I have a gun with me, and things will go according to plan." He said that he'd make sure that he had the best. "Good. It's what I deserve after all the shit that's been going on lately."

She didn't know what they were talking about, but continued to listen. Maybe she could turn them in to the police, and that would be the end of their life around her. The more she thought about them being out of her life, the more she liked it. They'd been nothing but trouble since she'd been born, and they were only getting worse. She wanted to cry again when she was kicked in the leg by Tommy.

"Get up and fix me something to eat." She told him again that she didn't have enough for herself, much less him, too. "I don't give a shit, Raven. I said to get up and fix me something to eat, and I don't want that shit you were eating either. I want something good."

"It's all I have. I told you that when you were here before." He pulled out a wad of cash and handed her a fifty. There was blood all over the money, and she didn't want to touch it. "What am I supposed to do with that?"

"Order something for me. And it had better be enough for just me. You can go on having your own meal." She decided that she was going to wash the money off before she called anyone. There was no telling what sort of trouble she'd cause if she were to hand it over to someone who came to the door.

Before You Go...

HELP AN AUTHOR

write a review

THANK YOU!

Share your voice and help guide other readers to these wonderful books. Even if it's only a line or two, your reviews help readers discover the author's books so they can continue creating stories that you'll love. Log in to your favorite retailer and leave a review. Thank you.

AWARD WINNING, BESTSELLING AUTHOR

Kathi S. Barton is an award-winning and bestselling author known for her steamy paranormal romances and unforgettable characters. A recipient of the prestigious Pinnacle Book Achievement Award, her books have topped the charts on Amazon and All Romance eBooks, earning her a loyal global readership.

Kathi lives in Nashport, Ohio, with her husband, Paul. When she's not crafting passionate love stories set in magical worlds, she enjoys camping, exploring local auctions, and attending county fairs, where Paul showcases his artwork and pottery. Her creative spark—fueled by a muse she describes as a cross between Jimmy Stewart and Hugh Jackman—brings her stories to vivid, heartfelt life.

Paranormal romance with plenty of heat is her favorite genre, and she loves connecting with her readers. Feel free to reach out—Kathi would love to hear from you.

Email: aaronskiss@gmail.com

Follow Kathi on her blog: http://kathisbartonauthor.blogspot.com/